There's Someone Out There.

A single footstep broke the silence behind her.

Talia didn't glance back. She took off running. She pumped her arms as hard as she could.

Footsteps pounded in her ears. Closer. Closer.

Close enough to whisper her name.

"Talia," the voicc said, as soft as the wind.

She cried out as she stumbled over something—a kid's small tricycle. She pitched forward, hitting the pavement hard.

Talia lay facedown on the sidewalk, panting, terrified.

Footsteps thudded onto the pavement . . . and stopped inches from hcr head.

All Talia could do was beg for mercy.

"Please!" she cried. "Please don't hurt me!"

Books by R. L. Stine

Fear Street

THE NEW GIRL
THE SURPRISE PARTY
THE OVERNIGHT
MISSING
THE WRONG NUMBER
THE SLEEPWALKER
HAUNTED
HALLOWEEN PARTY
THE STEPSISTER
SKI WEEKEND
THE FIRE GAME
LIGHTS OUT
THE SECRET BEDROOM
THE KNIFE
PROM QUEEN
FIRST DATE
THE BEST FRIEND
THE CHEATER
SUNBURN
THE NEW BOY
THE DARE
BAD DREAMS
DOUBLE DATE
THE THRILL CLUB
ONE EVIL SUMMER

Fear Street Super Chiller

PARTY SUMMER
SILENT NIGHT
GOODNIGHT KISS
BROKEN HEARTS
SILENT NIGHT 2
THE DEAD LIFEGUARD

The Fear Street Saga

THE BETRAYAL
THE SECRET
THE BURNING

Fear Street Cheerleaders

THE FIRST EVIL
THE SECOND EVIL
THE THIRD EVIL

99 Fear Street: The House of Evil

THE FIRST HORROR
THE SECOND HORROR

Other Novels

HOW I BROKE UP WITH ERNIE
PHONE CALLS
CURTAINS
BROKEN DATE

Available from ARCHWAY Paperbacks

For orders other than by individual consumers, Archway Books grants a discount on the purchase of **10 or more** copies of single titles for special markets or premium use. For further details, please write to the Vice-President of Special Markets, Pocket Books, 1230 Avenue of the Americas, New York, NY 10020.

For information on how individual consumers can place orders, please write to Mail Order Department, Paramount Publishing, 200 Old Tappan Road, Old Tappan, NJ 07675.

The Thrill Club

A Parachute Press Book

AN ARCHWAY PAPERBACK
Published by POCKET BOOKS
New York London Toronto Sydney Tokyo Singapore

AN ARCHWAY PAPERBACK *Original*

An Archway Paperback published by
POCKET BOOKS, a division of Simon & Schuster Inc.
1230 Avenue of the Americas, New York, NY 10020

ISBN: 0-671-78581-8

First Archway Paperback printing May 1994

10 9 8 7 6 5 4 3

Cover art by Bill Schmidt

Printed in the U.S.A.

IL 7+

The Thrill Club

chapter
1

Shandel Carter shivered and glanced back quickly over her shoulder. Is it my imagination, she wondered, or is someone following me?

It must be my imagination.

But why was it so dark? And why weren't there any streetlights on this part of Fear Street? It was bad enough that she had to walk past the cemetery by herself. At least there could have been a little moonlight to keep her company.

Her sneakers thudded on the sidewalk as she hurried toward home. She listened again for footsteps behind her. But the only noise was that from her shoes and the shrill howl of a cat somewhere far in the distance.

Why am I walking home alone on Fear Street at this time of night? Shandel asked herself. She shook her head, frowning as she quickened her pace.

If only she and Nessa hadn't gotten into that stupid argument. Nessa could have given her a ride home, just like any other night.

But, no. Shandel shook her head, silently scolding herself. Why do I always have to be so stubborn? Why do I always have to be the one who's right?

Shandel couldn't even remember what had started the argument. She and Nessa were talking and laughing, as usual, pretending to do their homework. Somehow the conversation turned to the topic of ghosts.

"I saw one," Nessa told her casually. "Last night. I was walking past the Fear Street cemetery on my way home from Maura's house."

"Right." Shandel laughed. "A man with a meat cleaver. Wearing a hockey mask. I've seen that movie."

A dreamy look passed across Nessa Troy's face. She had dark brown hair pulled back in a ponytail behind a pretty, delicate face.

"No," she said softly. "It was a woman. A woman in a wedding dress. She floated up from the grave and stared at me for a couple of seconds. Then she disappeared."

"That's all?" Shandel was disappointed. "That's not much of a ghost story."

"It's not a story," Nessa insisted. "It was real. It happened to me."

Nessa turned her attention back to her math homework. She frowned at one of her answers and started to erase it.

Shandel felt herself getting angry. "Come on, Nessa. You don't expect me to believe that."

Nessa glanced up from her notebook. "Excuse me?"

"You don't *really* expect me to believe you saw a ghost, do you?"

"Of course I do. You're my best friend, Shandel. If you don't believe me, who will?"

Shandel didn't answer. Nessa returned to her notebook.

Shandel tried to work out a problem, but couldn't concentrate. Somehow the story had gotten under her skin. A ghost in a wedding gown. Why did it bother her so much? She reached across the table and plucked the pencil out of Nessa's fingers.

"Admit it," she said. "Admit you are making it up."

Nessa wouldn't budge. "I told you what I saw, Shandel. Now can I please have my pencil back?"

Shandel wrapped her fingers tightly around the pencil. She knew she was being childish. "Not until you admit you were making that story up."

"I wasn't." Nessa insisted. "So give me back the stupid pencil."

Nessa angrily snatched at the pencil, but Shandel was too quick for her.

Nessa glared at her across the table. "If you don't believe my story, you can just get out of my house."

"Okay," Shandel shot back. "I will."

And she had. She gathered up her books, grabbed her jacket, and stormed out the front door, still clutching Nessa's pencil in her hand. She stuffed it into her shoulder bag and started walking.

It wasn't a long walk. Her house was on Canyon Road, only ten minutes away. But why did it have to be so dark?

A breeze swirled, making the trees whisper. The air suddenly carried a chill. A heavy blanket of clouds hovered low, covering the moon.

As she approached the Fear Street cemetery with its old tombstones poking up from the ground like crooked teeth, Shandel spun around. She stared into the blackness behind her.

Something moved. A dark shape, ducking behind a tree trunk.

Just my imagination?

Maybe. Maybe not.

I don't want to hang around to find out!

Shandel sprinted down the street, clutching her shoulder bag like a football. If only I could run like this at a track meet, she thought, lengthening her stride to cover more ground. I'd probably make the state championships.

Almost past the cemetery, she finally stopped to catch her breath. One of her shoelaces was untied. She bent down to tie it.

As she stood up, Shandel froze.

What was that?

She held her breath and listened carefully. A voice. The softest whisper.

"Shandel."

Run, she urged herself. Run.

But her legs wouldn't move. They felt planted in the ground.

"Shandel," the voice whispered again. Playful, teasing.

"Nessa," she hissed, "if you're trying to scare me, I'll never ever forgive you."

Shandel turned her head in the direction of the whispers. They seemed to be floating out from the cemetery.

All at once, against the purple sky, she saw a dark cloud. Smoke. She stared in horror, watching it rise up from behind a tilted gravestone.

No. No way, she thought.

No way I'm standing here, watching this.

Please, please—don't let it be a ghost.

"Shandel."

The whisper. Right behind her. Right in her ear.

She gasped as something cold touched her neck. Something cold and sharp. The motion was quick and clean.

She felt the hot wetness before she felt the pain.

She reached up with both hands. When she brought them down, they were smeared with dark blood.

My throat, she realized. Someone cut my throat.

Her legs felt rubbery. Weak.

She dropped to her knees. The dark ground rose up to meet her.

"Ohhh." A low groan escaped her throat.

Her cut, bleeding throat.

She felt so warm and so cold—all at the same time.

Her shoulder bag burst open as it hit the sidewalk, spilling its contents.

My throat . . . I'm bleeding. Help me.

Shandel reached out blindly, groping for anything that might save her.

All she found was a pencil.

chapter 2

Talia Blanton finished reading the story and gazed around the room with her blue eyes. She could tell that her friends in the Thrill Club had enjoyed it.

The other five members of the club were sprawled around Seth Varner's small rec room. They wore dazed, thoughtful expressions. No one spoke.

I guess the story is a hit, Talia thought. She winked at Seth. He flashed her a quick smile.

"Wow." Rudy Phillips spoke first. His brown eyes sparkled with pleasure behind his gold wire-rimmed glasses. "That was awesome, Talia."

"It gave me chills. Really," Maura Drake chimed in. "I mean, I could *feel* the blood oozing down her neck."

Rudy let out a high-pitched giggle. He wrapped his hands around Maura's throat.

"Rudy—give me a break!" Maura squirmed out of his grasp. "Rudy is too young for these stories," she muttered. She frowned at him. "It's past your bedtime, isn't it?"

"I won't sleep tonight. Not after *that* story!" Rudy declared. He turned to Nessa, who was sprawled on the floor on the other side of the room. "Hey, Nessa—do you have a pencil I can borrow?"

Everyone laughed.

Nessa grinned at Rudy. "Since when did *you* learn how to work a pencil?"

"Ooooh! She got you, man!" Seth told Rudy, jumping up from the couch and slapping Rudy on the back.

"Maybe we should change this to a comedy club," Maura muttered. "We could all do stand-up routines."

"Know any good jokes?" Rudy asked, glancing around the room. "Know any dirty jokes?

"A pig fell in a mud puddle!" Nessa said. "That's a dirty joke."

"Ha-ha," Maura said sarcastically. "I haven't heard that one since I was five!"

"Let's talk more about Talia's story," Nessa suggested.

"Okay. What's the moral of the story?" Rudy asked, grinning.

"Never borrow a pencil from Nessa!" Seth chimed in.

Everyone laughed.

Nessa Troy shook her head. "No way. The *real* moral of the story is never doubt my word," she said, fingering a curl of her dark brown hair. "If I say I saw a ghost, then I saw a ghost."

"Boo!" Maura said, rolling her eyes.

Still standing at the front of the rec room, Talia listened as the other five club members all began talking at once. Starting the Thrill Club was a great idea, she thought. The six friends met every week at a different person's house to swap stories and frighten one another.

Talia took pride in being the writer in the group. She liked these moments best of all, when her stories had just ended. Everyone admired her, wondering how she turned out a scary story every week.

Everyone but Seth, of course. He knew her guilty secret. He knew that Talia hadn't had time to write lately.

So Seth had written the last few stories for her.

Shaking that thought from her mind, Talia suddenly noticed that one member of the club was strangely quiet.

"Shandel?" she asked. "Is something wrong?"

Shandel Carter sat by herself in the far corner of the room, her long legs flung over the arm of the easy chair. Seeing Shandel's tense expression, Talia felt a sudden twinge of remorse.

But it wasn't me, she reminded herself. I didn't write the story. Seth did.

"What's the matter?" she pressed Shandel. "Didn't you like the story?"

Shandel touched her neck, as if checking for blood. She was attractive, tall and slender, with high cheekbones and beautiful hazel eyes that were set off by her dark skin. She always wore her maroon and gray Shadyside High track team jacket.

"Like it?" Shandel's eyes widened in disbelief. "I *hated* it! Why do you have to use real names in your stories?"

Talia had asked Seth the same question when he showed her the story earlier in the evening. She had to finish a report for history so he had offered to write the story for her.

Now Talia gave Shandel the same answer Seth had given her. "Because it's scarier that way, don't you think?"

"Well, don't use my name anymore," Shandel warned her. "I don't like having my throat cut—even in a dumb story."

"Dumb?" Talia cried, feeling as if *she* had just been stabbed.

Shandel scowled at her. "You know what I mean," she muttered. "Just don't use my name, okay?"

"I think using real names in the story is cool," Maura chimed in. "I mean, it makes it more real. You can picture the person getting her throat slashed."

"I don't *want* to picture it!" Shandel insisted, grabbing her throat again.

Everyone laughed.

Talia gazed at Maura, unable to hide her surprise

that Maura had defended her. Maura was a chubby redheaded girl with wide green eyes and plenty of freckles on her plain round face.

Talia hadn't heard a kind word from Maura—not since Talia had started seeing Seth.

She wondered if Maura had finally gotten over Seth. Maybe Maura and I can be friendly again, Talia thought wistfully. Maybe we can stop bickering now.

But then she saw Maura smile at Seth. "Maybe I should compliment you on the story too!" she said slyly.

Seth pretended he didn't know what Maura meant.

Talia felt her face heat up. "Hey! What's that supposed to mean?"

Maura shrugged and ran her fingers slowly through her short copper-colored hair. Her only good feature, Talia thought cattily.

Talia's hair was much prettier—long, blond, and silky, a perfect complement for her clear blue eyes. She knew how pretty she was. And if Talia ever forgot, there were always lots of boys around to remind her.

"Hey, don't act so innocent, Talia," Maura said. "You mean Seth doesn't help with your stories—the way he helps with your math?"

"No way," Talia protested. "Every word in that story is mine. Every word! Tell her, Seth."

Seth sat close to Maura on the red vinyl couch. He was tall and thin, with wavy dark hair and an intense, handsome face. He shifted uncomfortably, crossing his long legs. "Uh—whatever," he conceded.

Very helpful, Talia thought bitterly. She wondered if he'd blabbed their secret to Maura. Some guys were like that. Always loyal to old girlfriends.

Sometimes Talia wondered why she put up with Seth. He seldom talked to her anymore, hardly ever kissed her. Some boyfriend.

All he does is my homework. Next week, she vowed, I'm going to write the story myself—if I get a good idea.

She smiled at Maura. "Okay, Maura, maybe my next story will be about *you.* Of course, you'll be the victim."

"Just make sure it's death by chocolate!" Maura joked.

Everyone laughed but Shandel, who climbed up from her chair and lazily stretched her long arms over her head. "Talia's on a power trip," she said.

"Shandel—what's your problem?" Talia shot back.

"Other people have feelings too, you know," Shandel complained. "You should remember that when you write these stories."

Talia glanced around the room. Everyone was watching her, waiting for her response. She tried to relieve the tension with a joke.

"What else is wrong with me?" she asked. "We can make a list of my faults, from A to Z."

"Who has the time?" Shandel cracked. "I have to be home by eleven!"

Maura burst out laughing. The others were grinning.

Talia felt herself getting irritated. She really hated to be laughed at.

Shandel pressed her advantage. "Let's see," she said, playfully scratching her chin. "Why don't we start with *A*. I think *annoying* begins with *A*."

"Hey—she can spell!" Talia replied sarcastically.

"I can think of one that starts with *B*," Maura added with a snicker.

Talia waited for someone to come to her defense, but no one did. Not even Seth. Some boyfriend, she thought again unhappily.

Nessa was still on the floor, her back against the wall. She leaned forward, grinning. *"Attack of the Thrill Club Members!"* she cried, laughing.

From her standing position, Shandel bent over from the waist and placed both palms flat on the floor, as if warming up for a race.

"*Aggravating* also starts with an *A*," she said, straightening up with a grin.

Talia took a deep breath and held it. Shandel was always sarcastic. She always acted a little tough. But this time she was going too far.

I've got to stop her before I lose it, Talia thought. What can I do?

Distractedly, she patted the pocket of her jeans. The solution came to her out of nowhere. The knife. She'd forgotten she had it.

This will stop Shandel.

Walking slowly, steadily, Talia crossed the room until she was face-to-face with Shandel. Then she reached into her pocket and pulled out the switchblade.

When the silver blade sprang out, Shandel's mouth dropped open. She raised both hands to protect herself.

"How about an apology?" Talia asked, raising the knife menacingly. "I think that also starts with an *A.*"

Talia didn't wait for Shandel to reply.

She raised the knife and plunged it into Shandel's chest, aiming for the heart.

Her aim was perfect.

chapter 3

A gasp of horror escaped Shandel's throat. Her eyes widened in disbelief.

Her arms shot straight out, then she staggered backward, holding her chest.

Behind her, Talia heard the startled cries of her friends.

She raised the knife high, showing off the gleaming silver blade—and started to laugh. "April fool!" she exclaimed gleefully.

Still breathing hard, Shandel gazed down at the front of her sweater. No blood.

"Hey—" she shouted, more startled than angry.

Laughing, Talia pressed the knife blade into the palm of her hand. Instead of breaking the skin, the blade disappeared into the knife handle.

"Whoa!" she heard Rudy cry. "It's a fake."

Talia pushed the knife into her own chest. She pulled it out and held it up. "The blade slips into the handle."

"Cool!" Rudy cried. He crossed the room, his hand outstretched. "Can I see it?"

Talia handed him the knife. She had bought it that afternoon in a card shop. It was the kind of knife they used onstage and in the movies. She'd had a feeling it would come in handy during that night's meeting.

Her friends were chattering and laughing about her little stunt. Shandel still looked dazed.

Pleased with her triumph, Talia suddenly felt strange.

Stabbing Shandel like that—it seemed so real.

A cold chill ran down her back. It could be so easy to *really* kill someone, she thought.

So easy. So fast.

What a strange feeling . . .

Talia glanced over at Shandel, who was still standing in the middle of the room, dazed but unhurt. She was holding her hand over the spot where the knife had struck, as if saying the Pledge of Allegiance.

Talia hoped she hadn't scared her friend too badly. She reached out to pat Shandel on the arm.

But Shandel jumped back. "Talia," she snapped, "you keep your hands off me. I mean it."

"What's the matter?" Talia teased. "This is the Thrill Club, Shandel. Can't you take a joke?"

"A joke?" Shandel shook her head. "You've got a really weird sense of humor."

"Shandel," Talia begged, "please don't be mad at me."

Shandel gave her a stern look, her wide almond-shaped eyes narrowing with cool anger. "You know me, Talia. I don't get mad. I get even."

In her usual role as peacemaker, Nessa tried to smooth things over. "Come on, guys. It's over. Can't we just forget about it?"

Staring at Talia, Shandel repeated in the same chilly tone, "Like I said. I don't get mad. I get even."

The meeting broke up a few minutes later. Shandel and Nessa left together. Talia walked them to the door, hoping Shandel would accept her apology. But Shandel offered Talia only a cold stare and a muttered "Later."

Her feelings hurt, Talia returned to the rec room to find Maura and Seth sitting close on the couch, talking in whispers.

Talia stared at them from the doorway. When Seth had started the Thrill Club a few months earlier, Talia remembered, he and Maura had been dating for a whole year.

But he had seemed eager to drop Maura. He kept asking Talia out until she finally agreed. She knew it would ruin her friendship with Maura—but she found herself drawn to Seth in a way she had never been to any other boy.

Talia watched them on the couch, Maura laughing, touching Seth lightly on the wrist.

Why don't I feel jealous? Talia wondered. Am I already tired of Seth?

Only two months before, she had really thought she was in love with him. Now she wasn't sure.

Seth had changed so much since the death of his father three weeks earlier. He seemed so distant sometimes. Almost like a stranger.

"Hey." Rudy's voice startled her. She'd forgotten he was in the room. He moved up beside her so quietly. "That was a great story," he told her. "Really. It gave me a major case of the creeps."

"Thanks," Talia replied uncomfortably.

Rudy smiled at her. He was shorter than Talia, but surprisingly muscular now that he'd started working out. And he had nice brown eyes, soft and curious behind his gold-rimmed glasses.

Talia had never really noticed them before. Rudy gave her the impression of being strong and gentle at the same time.

"I think you'll be famous one day," Rudy predicted. "Talia Blanton, best-selling horror author. People will line up to be frightened by your books."

"Really?" Talia was flattered. "Do you think so?"

"Sure." Rudy nodded.

He'd barely finished speaking, when Maura rushed across the room and grabbed Rudy by the arm. "What are you two talking about?" she demanded suspiciously.

"Nothing," Talia replied innocently. "Just talking about my story."

"Everyone was so stressed out tonight," Maura commented, holding on to Rudy and edging toward the door. "I don't get it."

Rudy glanced over his shoulder on the way out. "See you in school," he called.

"Not if I see you first!" Talia joked.

"It's old-joke night," she heard Maura mutter. They disappeared out the door.

Seth was still slouched on the couch, staring glumly at his sneakers. Now it's just the two of us, thought Talia.

She sat down next to him and took his hand. She wished there were something she could do to cheer him up. He used to love practical jokes like that fake knife. He and Talia would sit and laugh for hours about the dumbest things.

These days, he seemed glum and distracted almost all the time.

"Are you okay?" she asked softly.

"Yeah. I'm fine," he replied defensively.

Talia shrugged. "You just seemed so quiet tonight."

Seth didn't answer. She hated when he got this way, so distant and distracted. Like she didn't exist. She took his hand and wrapped her fingers in his.

"Everyone loved the story you wrote for me," she murmured. "It was great of you to help me out."

"I don't mind," he said, giving her hand a gentle squeeze. "I had fun with it."

Talia felt a vague sense of guilt. Seth had written the last three stories for her. She'd been busy with other things, and he didn't seem to mind.

But now she was worried. Especially since the

other club members were beginning to suspect. She didn't want to lose her place as the writer in the group.

"You didn't tell Maura you wrote the story, did you?" Talia asked, not intending to sound shrill.

Seth pulled his hand away. "Hey—no way."

"Good." She felt relieved. "Maura really hates me, I think. I mean—"

Seth interrupted her by leaning close and kissing her softly on the lips. It was a pleasant surprise. She wanted the kiss to last, to remind her of the fun they had had before Seth changed.

He's so handsome, she thought. She loved the way his dark, curly hair fell across his forehead, the way his whole face lit up when he smiled. Back when he used to smile.

We used to be so happy. . . .

As if he could read her mind, Seth pulled away from her. His eyes focused off in the distance.

"Seth?" Talia waved her hand in front of his face. "Are you there? Is something wrong?"

He nodded slowly. His voice trembled. "I can't help it. I keep thinking about my father."

She felt awful. Selfish. Of *course* Seth wasn't himself. His father had died so recently.

"I'm really sorry," she murmured.

"There—there was something I didn't tell you," he said hesitantly. It was as if a shadow of sadness passed across his face.

She waited for him to continue.

"I was the one who found him. He was just sitting at his desk. Sitting straight up as if he were alive. This weird tape was playing on his cassette player. Very loud."

Seth took a deep breath. He let it out slowly, then continued. "I saw him sitting there in front of the tape player. I—I went up to talk to him and he—he didn't answer. I moved closer. His eyes were open, but he wasn't breathing. That's when I realized he was gone. I called for an ambulance, but it was too late."

"Have they figured out what he died of?" Talia asked softly.

Seth shook his head. "It's a mystery, Talia. A total mystery. The doctors—the coroner—no one could figure it out. Finally they just said natural causes."

"That's so awful." The words sounded awkward. But Talia didn't know what to say.

"There's more," Seth continued, avoiding her eyes. "The bad news doesn't end."

"What else?" Talia asked hesitantly.

"Mom says we're broke. Dad didn't leave us anything. We may have to move out of this house. Do you believe it?"

"I'm really sorry." Talia stroked his arm, trying to comfort him. "Things will get better," she said.

"They'd better!" Seth exclaimed. His expression changed suddenly. He jumped up from the couch. "I want to show you something," he said, narrowing his eyes. "Something very strange."

Talia followed Seth upstairs to his bedroom on the second floor. They walked softly to avoid disturbing Mrs. Varner, who had fallen asleep on the living room couch. According to Seth, she had been unable to sleep in her own room since her husband died.

Seth's room was small but neat, barely large enough for his bed, desk, and dresser. He had a poster of a basketball player on one wall. His guitar leaned against the closet door.

Talia stared at the framed photograph on his dresser top. It was a snapshot of her and Seth, taken before a school dance. It was a funny photograph. They were both grinning like fools, mugging for the camera.

Turning from the dresser, Talia realized that she could see into the bedroom of the house next door. The curtains were open and a light was on. Talia saw someone moving around.

Seth pulled a cassette out of his desk drawer. "I'm going to play a tape for you," Seth told her solemnly.

"A tape? You mean music?"

"No." He concentrated on sliding the cassette into the player.

Just then a face appeared in the window of the house next door. Talia gasped in surprise. She squinted hard, trying to see more clearly.

It didn't seem possible.

"Seth—look. It's Maura," she whispered in alarm. "Is she spying on us? What's she doing there?"

chapter 4

Talia grabbed Seth's sleeve. "What is Maura doing there, Seth?" she whispered.

"She lives there," Seth replied calmly. "Didn't you know we were next-door neighbors?"

Talia shook her head. "I knew Maura lived on your block, but I missed the meeting at her house. I definitely didn't know you could see right into her window. That's totally weird."

"Actually," he said, "it was really cool when we were going together. We could stay in our rooms and talk all night if we wanted to. But now it's a little strange."

Talia stared out the window again. Her eyes met Maura's. Maura waved.

Talia didn't wave back. She walked over to the window and pulled down Seth's shade. Good night, Maura, she thought.

Talia felt herself growing impatient. It was getting late, and she and Seth hadn't even touched their math homework yet.

She moved away from the window. Seth had loaded the cassette into his boom box. "Seth—I don't have time for music," she said. "We have to—"

"It's my father's tape," he interrupted. "This is what he was listening to the night I found him at his desk. Look at this."

He handed her the clear plastic case. Talia squinted at the label. There were two words on it, written in Dr. Varner's microscopic printing: TRANSFER TAPE.

"Transfer tape? What's that supposed to mean?"

"You've got to hear it," Seth said solemnly. "It's so weird." Seth had a strange gleam in his eye that made Talia nervous. "You know my dad was an anthropologist at the university, right? Well, he was working with a primitive tribe in New Guinea just before he died."

He pressed a button and the tape began to play. Talia heard chanting voices. Deep voices and shrill ones, chanting together in a steady, machinelike rhythm.

"The voices don't sound human," she whispered. "The sounds all keep repeating, over and over."

"Shhh." Seth raised a finger to his lips. "Just listen."

He closed his eyes and seemed to fall into a dreamy trance.

Talia watched his lips moving soundlessly. What was he doing? Was he joining in the chant?

Seth was starting to worry her.

The strange voices grew louder. The rhythm picked up, faster, faster.

Talia's head started to pound. She suddenly felt dizzy.

I can't take much more of this, she thought. She covered her ears, but her hands couldn't block out the chanting voices. She tugged on Seth's sleeve, but he didn't open his eyes. His lips were moving silently, in time with the rapid chant.

"It's driving me crazy! Shut it off!" she screamed.

Seth didn't seem to hear her.

"Seth! Seth—please!"

Still no response.

Frantically, Talia grabbed him by the shoulders with both hands and started to shake him.

"Seth? Seth? Can you hear me? Are you *okay?*"

chapter

5

"Huh?"

Seth slowly opened his eyes.

Talia let go of his shoulders. "Seth—the music—you didn't hear me—you—" Talia stammered.

He gazed at her, his mouth forming an *O* of surprise. He seemed startled to find Talia in his room. "What is it? What do you want?"

"Seth!" she said sharply. "Turn the tape off—please! It's horrible! I hate it. I really hate it."

Talia's head throbbed as she started walking home. That horrible chanting. Those ugly voices. It was like a bad dream, she thought.

Why did Seth make her listen to it? Why does he listen to it?

She glanced at her watch. It was late, and she hated walking alone on Fear Street. Seth usually drove her home, but he wasn't feeling well after he helped her with the math and then listened to that awful tape again.

Talia didn't argue. She could see he was sick. It wouldn't kill her to walk home for once.

The old trees whispered above her as she walked. The houses were all dark. A pale mist hung over the low half-moon, like a thin curtain holding back the light. The dewy, dark lawns shimmered under the pale, filtered light.

Every few steps Talia stopped and glanced over her shoulder, certain that someone was following her.

No one there.

The wind made a tall hedge shudder.

Her sneakers scraped the pavement. She began walking faster.

Calm down, she urged herself. You've walked here a million times.

But Fear Street was Fear Street. There were so many horrifying stories told about the street. Talia didn't believe them. But just the same, she wished Seth lived on some other street.

As she approached the cemetery, she felt a tingling at the back of her neck. She stood completely still and listened, staring straight ahead into the darkness.

A single footstep broke the silence behind her.

She thought of her story. Seth's story. The image of Shandel lying on the ground, groping for a pencil, flashed through her mind.

The thought tightened her throat, gripped her in fear, and her heart began to race.

Talia didn't glance back.

She took off running. But her legs felt heavy. She could barely make them move.

What's wrong with me? What's wrong? she asked herself frantically.

The footsteps were louder now. Closer.

She pumped her arms as hard as she could.

Move! she commanded herself. *Move!*

She could feel icy sweat on her hot forehead. Her lungs ached with every step.

Footsteps pounded in her ears. Closer. Closer. Her pursuer was gaining on her.

Close enough to whisper her name.

"Talia," said the voice, as soft as the wind.

Do something! she told herself. *I've got to do something!*

Then she remembered the knife. It wasn't real, but her pursuer wouldn't know.

My only chance.

As she ran, she jammed her hand into her jeans pocket. She pulled out the trick knife.

She flicked open the switchblade.

She raised her arm, readying it.

"Oh!" She cried out as she stumbled over something—a kid's small tricycle. She pitched forward, hitting the pavement hard.

The knife flew out of her hand. She watched it land in a clump of low shrubs near the cemetery fence.

Talia lay facedown on the sidewalk, panting, terrified.

Footsteps thudded onto the pavement—stopped inches from her head.

All Talia could do was beg for mercy.

"Please!" she cried. "Please don't hurt me!"

chapter 6

"Please—" Talia cried, her shrill voice trembling. "Please—"

"Come on," said a familiar voice. "You can get up now."

Oh, no, thought Talia. It can't be.

"Talia," said the voice. "Let me help you up."

Talia reached out for the hand extended to her and picked herself up from the sidewalk. She didn't know whether to be relieved or furious.

"Now our meeting of the Thrill Club can be officially adjourned," Shandel said cheerfully. "This was payback for using my name in tonight's story. And for your little stunt with the knife."

Talia brushed dirt off her knees. She wasn't hurt, just scared and embarrassed. "Well," she murmured, "I guess we're even now."

"You guess?" Shandel didn't sound satisfied.

"That thing with the knife wasn't funny, Talia. It was really hostile. You really frightened me."

Maybe Shandel was right. The joke had gone kind of far, even for the Thrill Club.

"I'm really sorry," Talia told her. "Do you accept my apology?"

Talia waited. She was relieved when Shandel finally nodded.

"Seeing that I just scared *you* half to death," Shandel said, chuckling, "I guess it's okay. I forgive you."

Walking together, they made their way quickly past the cemetery. Talia's heart was still pounding.

After a minute or two had passed, Shandel broke the silence. Her voice was sympathetic. "You should have killed *Maura* in your story—not me. Did you see the way she was gazing at Seth with those goo-goo eyes?"

"I saw," Talia assured her. "What's the story with Maura and Rudy anyway? Are they having problems?"

Maura's so plain, Talia thought cruelly. I wonder what Rudy sees in her. He's a really nice guy. Cute too. Those big brown eyes. Those broad shoulders. Maura doesn't deserve a guy like him.

"You know Maura," Shandel said with a shrug. "She never really got over Seth. I hate to say it, Talia, but it wasn't right of you to break them up."

"I didn't," Talia cut in quickly. "Seth asked *me* out. I didn't break them up."

Shandel ignored her protests. "You don't even seem to care all that much about Seth," she said.

"That's not true," Talia protested. "Seth means a lot to me. We're really good together."

Even as she said it, Talia realized that she wasn't telling the truth. She and Seth didn't have a good relationship, not anymore. Seth was too distant, too wrapped up in his own problems.

"Hey, it's none of my business," Shandel continued, "but you and Seth—you're not going to make it as a couple."

"That's right," Talia snapped. "It's none of your business."

They walked the last couple of blocks in uncomfortable silence.

The wind, cold for spring, pushed against them. The curtain of mist darkened over the moon.

Talia stopped in front of her house. "Well," she said stiffly, "thanks for walking with me."

Shandel nodded and started away without even saying goodbye.

Talia was startled by the strong feeling of anger that swept over her. Anger she had never felt toward Shandel before.

What's going on? Talia asked herself. Shandel is my friend. She always talks like that. She always says what's on her mind.

So why do I suddenly feel such frightening anger?

Talia felt edgy, stressed out, when she woke the next morning. She hadn't slept well. Those crazy chants on Seth's tape had haunted her dreams.

Frightening dreams.

She was being chased through a maze by people she couldn't see. Dogs barked. Everything was noisy and terribly confused. All she knew was that she couldn't let herself get captured.

Now Talia felt exhausted, as if she'd been running all night long.

I'm not myself, she thought.

When she finally managed to drag herself downstairs, her mother was sitting at the kitchen table, looking perfect. As usual. My mom the lawyer, Talia thought. Never a wrinkle in her tasteful suits. Never a hair out of place.

"Well, well," said Mrs. Blanton, "look who finally decided to grace us with her presence."

"Yup," muttered Talia. "Lucky you."

Talia opened the refrigerator and pulled out the carton of orange juice.

"You can have eggs for breakfast, honey," Mrs. Blanton informed her. "Or how about some waffles?"

"Neither," said Talia. "I don't feel like eating this morning."

"You have to eat breakfast," her mother insisted. "It's the most—"

"Important meal of the day," Talia cut in, finishing her mother's sentence. "I know."

"I know I'm being a parent. But without breakfast, people can't function," Mrs. Blanton said with a sunny smile. "It's a simple fact of nature."

So Talia forced herself to eat two toaster waffles drowned in syrup. Then she trudged back upstairs, took a quick shower, and slipped into her most comfortable pair of jeans and an oversize green sweater. She usually wore dressier clothes to school, but didn't feel like making the effort now.

She put on some lipstick and smiled into the mirror. A pretty, cheerful-looking girl smiled back, her face framed by silky blond hair.

Well, she thought, at least I don't *look* like a wreck.

As usual, Talia didn't have much to say to her mother during the ten-minute drive to school. They were close, but Talia just wasn't a morning person. She never really felt like herself until lunchtime.

Her mother knew this from long experience and left Talia to her own thoughts. Talia's brother, Dave, now a sophomore at Duke, had been exactly the same way.

Mrs. Blanton smiled as they pulled up in front of the main entrance to Shadyside High. "Have a good day, Tally. I'll be in court all day, and then I have to go into the office. But I should be home by six."

"Okay," Talia replied absently. "I mean, see you."

What is *wrong* with me? Talia wondered, walking slowly up the path to the double doors. Why do I feel so totally wiped out?

As Talia entered the building, her heart sank. I don't want to be here, she thought. I just want to be home in bed.

To make matters worse, she turned a corner and

spotted Seth standing by her locker, waiting like a faithful dog.

I can't deal with him, she thought. Not now. I just don't want to talk to him.

Before he saw her, Talia ducked around the corner and out of sight. She used to look forward to seeing Seth first thing in the morning. But now she wasn't so sure.

When Seth wasn't being aloof, he followed her around like an annoying little brother. With Seth, it was either too much or too little. When she didn't feel ignored, Talia found herself being smothered.

And right now she had to find room to breathe.

What was she going to do about Seth? Dump him? Keep trying with him? Sit him down and have another heart-to-heart with him?

Should she tell him how unhappy she was with the way things were between them?

She couldn't decide. It would be cruel to break up with him now, when he was still so upset about his father.

Talia decided she'd just have to wait a little while longer, until he was strong enough to handle it.

She made her way back to her locker. Seth was nowhere in sight.

Two girls she knew—Jade Smith and Deena Martinson—called to her. She waved back, then concentrated on opening her locker. She just didn't feel like talking to anyone.

She felt a little better by the time homeroom ended and she entered her math class. Her mother was probably right about the waffles. She took her seat next to Nessa and set her notebook on her desk.

"Hi," said Nessa.

"Says you," Talia replied with a frown.

"What's your problem?" Nessa asked.

Talia shrugged. "Bad night."

In the front of the room, Mr. Hanson cleared his throat. Chairs scraped. Notebooks were opened. The chattering stopped.

"Talia," the teacher said, "I need to speak to you."

"Huh?" Talia wasn't sure she had heard correctly.

His expression was solemn. He didn't sound happy.

Talia glanced quickly at Nessa, who had turned to whisper something to Maura. Maura's eyes were wide with surprise. Something is wrong, Talia thought, getting up unsteadily from her chair.

On the way to the teacher's desk, Talia passed Rudy and Seth. Rudy flashed her a sympathetic look. Seth had his head down, pretending to double-check a homework problem.

Talia stood nervously in front of Mr. Hanson and tried to smile. "Yes?" she asked. "Is something wrong?"

Mr. Hanson didn't return the smile. He was a balding, pink-faced man with tortoiseshell glasses. As far as Talia could tell, he owned only two suits, one blue and one gray, and wore them on alternate days. Today it was the blue one.

"Outside," said Mr. Hanson, rising from his chair. "I need to talk to you in private."

When they stepped into the hallway, Mr. Hanson handed her a sheet of paper. Yesterday's homework.

Talia winced. Seth had done it for her while she watched TV. Never again, she thought.

"Tell me honestly," the teacher said, watching her closely with suspicious eyes. "Is this your work?"

"Of course it is." Talia tried to sound convincing, but her voice came out shrill and shaky.

He stared hard at her, his blue-gray eyes narrow through the thick eyeglasses. "You're sure?"

Talia nodded. "I'm sure. I'm not a cheater, Mr. Hanson."

He took the paper back from her. "You've always been a good student," he said softly. "Don't disappoint me."

Mr. Hanson opened the door, and Talia followed him back into the classroom. She could feel her face blazing, and knew that she was blushing.

She kept her eyes straight ahead as she walked back to her seat, trying to pretend that everything was all right.

She sat down and looked around the room, wondering if someone had snitched on her. But why? she wondered. Why would anyone want to get me in trouble?

Rudy stared at her from across the room, looking concerned. Seth kept his attention glued to his homework. Maura and Nessa traded whispers.

Then Talia's eyes came to rest on Shandel. She was sitting in the third row, wearing white overalls over a pink bodysuit, and staring straight back at Talia.

Shandel had the strangest smile on her face.

"I don't get mad," Talia remembered her saying. "I get even."

chapter 7

Nessa couldn't understand it. It was five after seven, and only one member of the Thrill Club had arrived at her house for the meeting. Ordinarily, one or two kids might show up late—usually Maura and Talia—but *four?* It was definitely weird.

"I don't get it," she told Rudy. "Where do you think everyone is?"

Rudy put down the *National Geographic* he'd picked up from the coffee table and gave a quick shrug. "I knew Maura would be late," he said, "because she called to tell me. But who knows where Talia, Seth, and Shandel are?"

"I really hate waiting around," Nessa complained. "If a meeting is supposed to start at seven, it should start at seven. I mean, I've got at least two hours of homework to do when this is over."

"Tell me about it," Rudy murmured. He sighed wearily. "I've got three chapters of history to read before that test on Friday."

"Ugh," said Nessa, rolling her eyes. "Don't remind me."

A few more minutes passed. Nessa took a nail file out of her purse and began giving herself a manicure. Rudy picked up another issue of *National Geographic.*

"Maybe they rang the doorbell and we didn't hear it," he suggested.

Nessa shook her head. "My parents are in the den upstairs. They'd definitely hear the doorbell."

As Nessa studied her nails, she thought back to her phone conversation with Shandel a half hour earlier. Shandel had sounded excited. She said she had a secret she wanted to tell Nessa. Nessa was dying to find out what it was.

"This isn't like Shandel," Nessa remarked. "She's always on time. It's not like Seth to be late either."

"Let's give them a few more minutes," Rudy suggested. "If no one shows up in ten or fifteen minutes, we can start making phone calls."

Nessa nearly jumped off the couch when the doorbell rang. *Finally,* she thought. Now we can get started.

She hurried up the basement steps, through the hallway, and opened the front door. Maura stood smiling on the porch, her short red hair gleaming wet.

"Sorry I'm late," she said. She tugged at her wet hair. "I had to shower."

"You're only the third one here," Nessa told her. "It's just you, me, and Rudy."

"Really?" Maura squinted in surprise as she stepped into the hallway. "Where are the others?"

"Good question," Nessa replied. "I wish I knew."

They made their way downstairs and joined Rudy in the basement. He had put down the *National Geographic* in favor of a *Sports Illustrated.*

Nessa chuckled to herself as she reached for her nail file. She and her sister teased her father that the rec room was like a doctor's office, with all the magazines spread out on the coffee table.

"I bet I know where Talia is," Maura teased, plopping down on the couch next to Rudy. "She's probably at Seth's, waiting for him to finish her new story on his computer. Maybe the disk crashed or something."

"Maura, give us a break," Rudy said. There was a harsh note in his voice that made Nessa glance up from her nails. "Please don't start in on that again," he groaned.

"Why not?" Maura returned with a smile, her green eyes flashing with mischief. "Whose side are you on anyway? Mine or Talia's?"

Not wanting to get involved, Nessa lowered her eyes and pretended to be engrossed in her manicure.

"I'm on your side, Maura," Rudy quickly assured her.

Good answer, Nessa thought to herself. Her nails looked perfect, but she kept filing away, just to have something to do.

"Seth lets Talia take complete and total advantage of him," Maura continued, her tone more serious. "He does her homework, drives her around, and tags along behind her like a little lapdog. She treats him like a slave and he just begs for more. Some guys are just so—pitiful."

Nessa couldn't help herself. The psychology of boys was the one subject on which she considered herself an expert. After all, she'd devoted a great deal of time and effort to the topic.

"The way I see it," she told Maura, "if Talia treats Seth like a slave, it's only because he lets her. And if he lets her, he must enjoy it. So who are we to get on his case? Or her case?"

"Oh, great." Maura rolled her eyes. "Thanks for the expert analysis."

Nessa started to reply, but stopped when she heard the basement door opening. Footsteps pounded down the stairs.

She turned to see Seth enter the rec room, dressed in black jeans and a camouflage T-shirt, his outfit of choice since the death of his father. He nodded and sat down in a metal folding chair.

"Hey," said Nessa. "Who let you in?"

"Your dad," replied Seth. "He was sitting on the porch, smoking his pipe. He said your mom won't let him smoke in the house."

"Yeah," said Nessa. "My mom's pretty strict about that."

"Sorry I'm late," Seth told her. "My mother asked me to do the dishes." His eyes narrowed as he glanced around the room. He glanced at his watch. "Hey, where are Talia and Shandel? It's almost twenty after seven."

"It's weird," said Nessa. "Shandel's never late. You'd think she would've called by now."

Rudy turned to Seth. "Did Talia tell you she was going to be late?" he asked.

Seth ran his fingers through his wavy hair. He seemed to be searching his mind for an answer. "No," he said after a brief hesitation. "I talked to her after school, and she just said she'd see me at the meeting. She said she was working on a new story."

"That's a good one," Maura said, then laughed.

"What's so funny?" asked Seth.

Nessa rose impatiently from her chair. "I'm calling Shandel," she said. "I'm sick of waiting."

Nessa had walked to the foot of the stairs when she heard the basement door open again. Talia came rushing down the steps, her face flushed, her expression tense.

"It's me," Talia said breathlessly, pushing stray wisps of blond hair out of her eyes. "I'm really sorry."

"What happened?" Nessa asked. "Where were you?"

Talia frowned. She stared hard at Nessa without replying.

"I—I don't know," she said finally, shaking her

head in confusion. "I guess I just lost track of time."

Talia felt groggy, as if she had just awakened from a nap.

Nearly seven-thirty! How could that have happened?

She had left her house twenty-five minutes ago! And it was only a ten-minute walk from her house to Nessa's, fifteen minutes at the most.

What's wrong with me? she wondered.

"Is everything okay?" Nessa asked her.

"Yeah. I'm fine," Talia answered. "I'm just trying to catch my breath."

"Can I take your sweatshirt?" offered Nessa.

Talia glanced down at the wadded-up white sweatshirt in her hand. She couldn't remember taking it off.

Why am I carrying it? she wondered.

"That's okay," she told Nessa, tightening her grip on the sweatshirt. "I'll just hold on to it."

Nessa gave her a puzzled look. "It's okay, Talia. I'll put it in my room with Maura's jacket. I'm going up there anyway. I have to call Shandel's house to find out what's taking her so long."

Talia snapped out of her daze long enough to glance around the rec room. "Shandel's not here?" she asked, reluctantly surrendering the sweatshirt to Nessa.

Nessa shook her head. "I can't believe she hasn't called," she complained, slipping past Talia on her way upstairs. "Shandel's usually more thoughtful than this."

Talia felt a little better now that she realized she wasn't the only person late for the meeting. She sat down on a folding chair next to Seth. She said hi to Rudy and Maura.

Seth reached out and took her hand. He leaned closer, bringing his mouth to her ear. "How's it going? Everything okay?" he whispered. His voice was soft, reassuring. "I was getting worried about you."

"I—I think so," Talia whispered back.

"What happened?" he asked. "Why are you so late?"

Talia hesitated. I don't know what happened, she thought to herself. But how could she explain that, even to Seth?

"Nothing," she replied. "I just lost track of time."

Rudy closed the magazine on his lap and dropped it onto the coffee table. "I can't wait to hear your new horror story," he told Talia.

Before Talia could tell him that she hadn't been able to write one, Nessa came back down the stairs, shaking her head fretfully.

"Something's wrong," she announced. "I just talked to Shandel's mother. She said Shandel left the house nearly a half hour ago. And it's only a short walk from her house to here."

"I'm sure she'll be here any minute," said Maura. "Maybe she stopped to get some chips or something."

"Why don't we go look for her?" Rudy suggested, rising from the couch. "It's better than sitting around here, filing our nails," he added, smiling slyly at Nessa.

"Good idea," agreed Seth. "My car's outside. All five of us can fit."

Maura jumped up from the couch and turned her gaze to Talia. "Let's go," she said impatiently. "What are we waiting for?"

"Fine," said Talia.

In single file, the group clumped up the carpeted staircase to the hallway. All the way up the stairs, Talia felt Maura's hard gaze drilling into her back. What's Maura's problem? she wondered again.

Maura stopped by the front door, tapping herself on the forehead, as if she'd just remembered something. "I'll meet you at the car," she told the others. "I have to run upstairs to get my jacket."

"Could you get my sweatshirt too?" Talia asked her. "Nessa said she put it in her room."

"Sure," said Maura. She disappeared up the stairs.

Talia followed the others outside. Darkness hadn't yet fallen. A pale crescent moon hung in the graying sky, and a cool breeze rushed through the treetops.

Talia shivered in her T-shirt. When is it going to start feeling like spring? she wondered.

"You want to sit up front?" Seth asked her.

"That's okay," said Talia. "I'm happy to squeeze in the back."

"I'll sit in the front," Nessa said eagerly, pulling

open the door and climbing into the front seat. "My whole life, I've been riding in the back."

Rudy climbed in back. Talia stood alone on the sidewalk, rubbing her arms against the chill. A few seconds later Maura came jogging down the sidewalk with Talia's white sweatshirt. "Here you go," she said, tossing it to her.

Talia pulled the sweatshirt over her head, taking care not to mess up her hair. It felt a lot better to have something warm on. "Thanks," she told Maura.

But Maura didn't answer.

Her eyes widened as she gaped at Talia's sweatshirt.

"What—what's wrong?" Talia stammered.

Maura pointed to a large, dark smear down the right sleeve of the sweatshirt.

"Talia," she cried. "How did you get that bloodstain?"

chapter 8

With a startled gasp, Talia stared down at her sleeve.

A mysterious reddish brown smudge ran down to the white cuff of her sweatshirt.

Was it a bloodstain?

Where did it come from? She blinked her eyes and examined it again.

"Did you cut yourself?" Rudy asked out the open backseat window.

"I don't think so," she replied uncertainly.

"Maybe you had a nosebleed," he suggested. "I get them sometimes at night, when I'm sleeping. I don't even realize it until I wake up, and the pillow's covered with blood."

Talia cringed at the thought of a bloody pillow. "Maybe," she said doubtfully. She hadn't had a nosebleed in years. "It's probably just dirt."

"Looks like a bloodstain," Maura said, narrowing her eyes at the sweatshirt sleeve.

Nessa rolled down the passenger window. "Can we get going?" she called out impatiently. "Let's go find Shandel."

Before climbing into the car, Talia pushed the sleeves of the sweatshirt up past her elbows. That way she wouldn't have to see the bloodstain or answer any more questions. Then she lowered herself into the backseat between Maura and Rudy.

Seth started the engine of his mother's station wagon and made eye contact with Talia in the rearview mirror. He seemed to be watching her closely.

"Here we go," he said, pulling away from the curb. "The Thrill Club on patrol."

"We'll probably find Shandel after driving half a block," Maura said, staring hard out her window.

"I hope so," Nessa said tensely. "It's just so odd that we haven't heard from her."

"I'll bet she met some friends and is yakking away," Rudy offered.

"This is the weirdest Thrill Club meeting we ever had," Seth said, stopping at a four-way stop sign.

"Maybe we should just skip the meeting and go for pizza," Rudy suggested, rubbing his stomach. "It's been at least an hour since I ate."

Maura laughed. "You're such a pig."

"I am not," Rudy insisted. "I'm still growing, that's all."

The others remained tensely quiet.

Seth guided the car onto Canyon Road, past large

houses with rolling expanses of lawn and two- and three-car garages. "It isn't even hilly here," he remarked. "Why do you think they called it Canyon Road?"

"Probably named it after Mr. Canyon," Rudy joked.

"Where's Shandel?" Nessa demanded shrilly. "I really don't like this."

They drove on in silence, peering out at the dark houses and lawns rolling by. Even though it was still early, there were few cars on the street. And no one walking on the sidewalks.

It seemed as if they had just pulled away from Nessa's house when Seth announced, "Here we are."

He stopped the car in front of a big stone house with a silver Saab and a maroon minivan in the driveway.

Talia blinked her eyes. Had they already reached Shandel's?

"I don't like this at all," said Nessa. "I was sure we'd run into her on the way."

"I'll bet she took the cemetery shortcut," Talia suggested. "That's the way she and I walked home last week."

Nessa twisted in the front seat to look back at Talia. "I doubt it," she said. "The cemetery gives Shandel the creeps. She'd never walk past it by herself."

"Maybe she ran into someone," suggested Maura.

"Let's give it a try," Seth said decisively. He

turned the car around in front of Shandel's house, drove two blocks back down Canyon Road, then turned onto Fear Street and headed toward the cemetery.

"If we don't see her, we'll just go back to my house," Nessa said anxiously, staring hard into the darkness. "Maybe she got a ride or something. Maybe she's at my house, waiting for us."

Talia felt queasy as they approached the cemetery.

"I don't see her," Nessa said as they cruised past the black iron gate.

"Hold your breath!" Rudy cried, sucking in a deep breath.

"Rudy—what's your problem?" Maura demanded.

"You have to hold your breath when you go past a cemetery," he told her. "Otherwise, it's bad luck."

Maura glared at him sternly. "That's really dumb. Aren't you worried about Shandel?"

Talia's muscles tensed as she gazed out at the rows of headstones poking up along the sloping hill on the other side of the fence.

Suddenly Maura's eyes grew wide. "Hey—stop!" she cried. "Seth—stop. Go back!"

Seth hit the brakes hard, tossing them all forward.

"What? What is it?" Nessa cried shrilly.

"Look!" Maura shouted. She pushed open her car door and scrambled out.

Startled, Talia watched her run along the sidewalk onto the grass. Then she pulled herself out of the car to follow Maura.

They were all running along the cemetery fence now, running breathlessly, following Maura.

They stopped when they heard Maura's first scream.

"Noooooo!"

Maura's cry pierced the heavy silence.

And then she began to wail: "No! No! Please—noooooooo!"

chapter 9

"Noooooo!" Nessa's cry sounded more like an animal howl.

"Nessa—what?" Seth uttered, running up to her.

Talia lagged behind, her heart pounding. She didn't want to see why Nessa was shrieking. She didn't want to see. . . .

By the time Talia caught up with the others, Nessa was sobbing loudly in Rudy's arms.

Talia stepped onto the wet grass, forcing herself to stare at the familiar human shape stretched out on the ground.

Oh, no, she thought.

Please, no.

Not Shandel.

Not my friend Shandel.

"Call an ambulance!" Maura shrieked wildly. "Find a phone! Someone—call an ambulance!"

Shandel lay sprawled facedown in the grass, her arms wide, as if she were hugging the ground. Talia stared at the white letters on the back of her team track jacket. They spelled TIGERS.

Seth squatted beside Shandel and squeezed her wrist, searching for a pulse. Shandel's arm hung limply when he lifted it off the ground.

Seth let out a low cry as he let the hand drop. He raised his eyes to the others. "She's dead," he murmured.

Maura uttered a shrill cry. Nessa sobbed loudly. Rudy was breathing hard, his chest heaving.

"L-look at her neck," Maura stammered, pointing in horror. "It—it's been cut. Someone cut her! Someone cut her!"

Talia leaped back from Shandel's body, as if someone had shoved her. A wave of nausea swept up from her stomach. She opened her mouth to scream, but no sound came out.

Her feet made a wet, squishy sound as she moved them on the sidewalk.

Talia stared down.

Then she screamed, long and loud.

Her new white sneakers were soaked red with blood.

The next half hour passed in a blur of flashing red and blue police and ambulance lights.

Talia couldn't seem to stop crying. Any thought of Shandel—her laughter, the way her mouth curled when she smiled—brought fresh tears flooding back into her eyes.

How could this happen? she asked herself. What kind of monster would cut someone's throat?

The ambulance pulled away. Talia felt Seth's hand fall softly onto her shoulder. When she turned, he was gazing at her with sad, understanding eyes. "The police want us all to come down to the station," he told her.

"Why?" she asked, trying to control her sobs.

"They want to ask us a few questions," he said. "They're just gathering information. About Shandel."

Talia nodded. I've got to pull myself together, she told herself.

"They're calling our parents," Seth continued. "They'll meet us at the police station."

Police station? I'm just a teenager, Talia thought. Why would I be at the police station?

My friend was murdered.

The words cut through her, sharp as a knife blade.

I have to go to the police station—because my friend was murdered.

Talia followed Seth across the street to the station wagon. Maura, Rudy, and Nessa were waiting in the backseat, their faces pale and tear streaked.

Seth started the engine, and they pulled away from the curb to follow a police cruiser with flashing lights. No one spoke until they turned into the lot behind the Shadyside Police Station.

"It's so strange," Nessa said, her voice trembling. "Shandel. The cemetery. It's all so much like Talia's last horror story."

"I know," agreed Maura with a shudder. "It's really creepy."

"Such an awful coincidence," Rudy muttered, shaking his head sadly.

Talia squirmed uncomfortably in the passenger seat, upset by the drift of the conversation. She had an impulse to confess that Seth had written the story for her. But she stopped herself.

Shandel's dead, she thought. That's the only thing that matters.

Talia's legs felt shaky and weak as she and her friends climbed out of the car. A tall police officer with blond hair and a mustache held open the station wagon door.

The police station was bright and modern looking. Talia shielded her eyes, waiting for them to adjust to the bright fluorescent light.

Then she saw her parents waiting by the front desk, along with Seth's mother and Maura's dad. She immediately burst into tears.

Two hours later Seth drove Talia home from the station, following her parents' car. Talia's mother and father had spoken to Shandel's parents and were very shaken.

Seth volunteered to drive Talia home so that he and she could be alone to talk. But Talia had been unable to utter a word.

Seth pulled up in front of Talia's house. They watched her parents disappear into the house. He turned off the engine and reached across the front seat to take her hand.

"Will you be okay?" Seth asked her.

"I—I think so," Talia replied in a weak voice. She felt guilty for the distance she'd put between Seth and herself the past few days. He'd been so wonderful all evening, so calm and supportive. "Thanks for being so helpful," she told him. "It's been a horrible night."

He nodded. A choked sob escaped his throat. "Horrible," he murmured.

"I hated having to answer all those questions," Talia said. "I kept thinking the police were trying to accuse me of something."

"Me too," Seth confessed. "I hated the way they kept repeating the same questions."

Talia nodded. She felt a cold chill run down her back.

The officer kept asking if Shandel had any enemies, if anyone had a grudge against Shandel, if anyone had ever threatened Shandel.

Talia wouldn't have been able to take it if her parents hadn't been there to help her out. Talia could see how careful the detective had been with his questions, knowing that Talia's mother was a lawyer.

"I wish Maura hadn't mentioned that horror story you wrote for me," Talia confessed. "I think that's why they questioned me for so long."

"Did you tell them I wrote it?" Seth asked. He had turned his face away from Talia to stare out the windshield.

"I wanted to," she said. "But it seemed more

trouble than it was worth. Do you think I should have?"

"It really doesn't matter," said Seth. "It wasn't your story that killed Shandel. It was a real person, with a real knife. The police will understand that."

Who murdered her?

The question forced its way into Talia's mind.

Who murdered her?

Someone Shandel knew?

A total stranger?

Someone in the Thrill Club?

No!

She started crying again. Seth slid across the front and wrapped his arms around her.

"Don't even think about that horror story," he whispered. "Don't even think about it. It's a stupid coincidence."

Talia wiped the tears from her eyes and nodded. Seth had been so strong all evening, so kind. She kissed him good night and ran her fingers through his wavy hair.

"I'd better go in," she told him. "My parents are waiting for me."

"Okay," he said. But before Talia could open the car door, Seth wrapped his arms around her once again and pressed his mouth to hers.

At first his lips were comforting and familiar, but then they became more passionate. She quickly warmed to his kiss.

He ended the kiss suddenly. Then he reached past her to open the door. "Call me tomorrow," he whispered.

Feeling confused and shaky, Talia climbed out. She shut the car door and walked slowly across the lawn and up the front steps.

Talia watched Seth drive away before she entered the house. Her parents stood tensely in the living room, waiting for her. Talia could see that her mother had been crying for Shandel too.

"Are you okay?" her father asked, crossing the room to her.

"I think so," she said uncertainly.

Her mother gasped as she glimpsed Talia's blood-soaked sneakers. "Why don't you go change into your pajamas," she suggested. "When you come down, I'll make some hot chocolate and we can talk."

Talia sighed wearily. "Okay," she agreed.

She trudged up to her room and kicked off her sneakers without touching them.

Then she crossed the room to her dresser. She pulled open the middle drawer and reached in for her nightgown.

Instead, she felt something cold, sharp, and wet.

"Huh?" She blinked, then gasped for breath as all the air seemed to leave her body.

Her chest heaving, the room tilting and swaying around her, she stared into the dresser drawer.

Stared at a knife.

Stared at the knife blade, covered with thick, sticky blood.

chapter 10

Talia didn't mention the knife to anyone for two days—until Seth came to pick her up for Shandel's funeral. She told him about it on the way to the memorial service.

Seth listened closely, his face tightening with concentration as he drove. "But why would somebody go to all that trouble?" he asked, braking for a red light. "I mean, what's the point of planting a knife in your drawer?"

"I don't know," Talia confessed, shaking her head. "I don't know, Seth."

"So what did you do with it?" he asked.

Talia tugged at the hem of her black dress. "I wrapped it in a newspaper and threw it in the garbage."

Seth glanced at her out of the corner of his eye. "Did you tell the police?"

"I was going to," Talia replied. "But I couldn't bear the thought of answering any more questions. Especially when I didn't have any answers."

She let out a long sigh. "I have no idea how the knife got there," she said, her voice barely above a whisper. "No idea at all. All I really know is that someone is trying to make me look like a murderer."

"But how could it have gotten into your drawer?" Seth asked.

Talia's face twisted in a thoughtful frown. "Maybe someone broke in while we were all at the police station that night and planted the knife in my drawer."

The traffic light changed. They started moving again. "Were there any signs of a break-in?" Seth asked.

"No," Talia replied softly. "But we leave a spare key under the welcome mat. Maybe the person who's trying to frame me used the key to get in."

"Well, then, it couldn't have been anyone from the Thrill Club," Seth said. "We were all at the police station too."

Seth remained silent for the last few blocks of the journey. He didn't say anything until they pulled into the crowded parking lot of St. Paul's Church.

"So what did it look like?" he asked, easing the car into one of the few remaining parking spaces. "Was it a big knife?"

"That's the weirdest thing," Talia told him. "The knife in my drawer—it looked almost like that joke knife I bought at the card store. But it was real."

She stepped out of the car and blinked her eyes against the strong morning sun. "Maybe someone's trying to drive me crazy. I really can't figure it out."

Seth put his arm around Talia's waist as they walked slowly through the lot and up the wide front steps of the church. "It doesn't make any sense," he told her, stopping in front of the heavy wooden door. "No one in the world would ever think that you killed Shandel."

"I—I don't know what to think," Talia confessed. She took Seth's arm after he lowered it and leaned against him.

He looked so somber and grown-up in his blue suit. The same suit he'd worn to his father's funeral little more than a month before.

Poor Seth, she thought. This can't be easy for him either.

"We'll get through this together," he whispered.

Talia wanted to hug him, but he'd already pulled open the door.

Talia felt trembly and self-conscious as they made their way slowly up the aisle and joined their friends, who were seated in the fifth row of dark wooden pews.

Rudy smiled in greeting. Maura made a point of not looking at Talia. Nessa was sobbing softly to herself, dabbing her eyes with a tissue.

Only seconds after Talia and Seth sat down, the minister took his place behind a podium at the altar. Four men in dark suits wheeled a closed coffin down the center aisle of the church.

Talia's throat tightened. She fought back a loud sob.

Is Shandel really in there? she asked herself, staring at the coffin shining under the bright chapel lights.

Why would anyone want to kill her?

And why would they want to make it look as if I did it?

Talia's mind kept spinning round and round, the questions, the unanswerable questions, repeating endlessly.

Talia's thoughts were interrupted by the muffled sound of sobbing from the front row. Shandel's mother had collapsed into her husband's arms. Her poor parents, Talia thought. It must be so awful for them.

"This has been the worst week of my life," Nessa wailed. "I can't believe Shandel's gone. I can't believe I'll go to school on Monday and not be able to eat lunch with her."

Nessa shook her head. Her eyes were swollen and glassy from crying. "Shandel was the best friend I ever had."

After the funeral, the five members of the Thrill Club had gathered at Alma's Coffee Shop. Talia felt completely drained, exhausted. All she could do was stare at her tuna sandwich.

With his fork, Rudy pushed his french fries from one side of the plate to the other. "I can't believe it either," he murmured.

"I can't believe somebody killed her," Maura said evenly. She raised her eyes to Talia. "I just keep wondering if it was someone who knew her."

Talia felt the blood rush into her face. Why is she staring at me? she wondered. What is Maura's problem?

"I haven't been able to eat since it happened," Talia said, lowering her eyes to the tuna sandwich.

"Me either," Nessa said sadly. She had a napkin in her hand and was shredding it into tiny pieces.

"It's so weird that Shandel died just like in Talia's story," Maura added.

Talia could feel her face burning under her friends' silent stares.

Rudy picked up his cheeseburger, opened his mouth, then lowered the burger back to his plate without biting into it. "Maura and I were talking last night," he told them. "We both agreed that it's probably a good idea to cancel next week's meeting."

"Yeah, right," Seth agreed, reaching across the table to spear a couple of Rudy's fries. "Maybe we should hold off until the week after."

Talia's mind drifted away from the conversation. She couldn't help replaying Shandel's funeral. Once again she saw the coffin sinking into the fresh grave, remembered the awful *thud* of dirt falling on top of the shiny coffin lid.

When Talia looked up, Maura was glaring at her again.

"Did you clean your sweatshirt?" Maura asked in a derisive tone of voice.

"Excuse me?" said Talia.

"The sweatshirt you wore the night of the murder. Did you clean the fresh bloodstain off your sweatshirt?" Maura repeated coldly.

chapter 11

Talia's throat tightened with anger—and fear.

Maura was definitely *accusing* her now.

Glancing around the booth, Talia realized everyone was staring at her, waiting for her answer. Think of something, she told herself. Think.

Her eyes moved quickly across the table, past the napkin holder and saltshaker, coming to rest on the bottles of condiments.

"It—it wasn't blood," Talia mumbled. "It was ketchup."

Talia stared at the phone. Saturday night.

Ring, she told it. Please ring. I don't want to sit here by myself. Not tonight.

She'd felt strange all day. Out of sorts. Lifeless.

She needed to get out of the house, do something fun to help her to forget her troubles.

All day she'd been looking forward to going out with Seth. So why didn't he call? He was usually so reliable.

In just a couple of days, Talia realized, a lot had changed between them. Earlier in the week she had been hiding from him, and seriously considering breaking up with him. Now she felt she needed him.

She rested her hand on the phone.

Ring, she pleaded. *Don't make me be alone tonight.*

Oh, well, she thought. I guess I'll have to call him. She picked up the phone and punched in his number.

Seth answered on the third ring. "Hello?"

"It's me," she said, trying to sound cheerful and casual. "Haven't you forgotten something?"

"Uh—what's that?"

"Aren't we going to the movies tonight?" Talia winced at the whiny sound of her voice. It sounded as if she were begging. "When are you picking me up?"

Seth hesitated. "I can't, Talia. I was just going to call you."

"But, Seth," she groaned. "We had a date."

"I know," he replied. "It's just that . . . well, something came up."

"Huh? Something came up?" What kind of lame excuse was that?

"My—my mother's not feeling well," he explained. "She's pretty sick. I don't think it's a good idea to leave her alone."

Talia didn't know what to say. She had a feeling he was lying, but of course she couldn't accuse him.

"I'm sorry," she said. "Do you want me to come over? We could watch TV or something."

"I don't think that's such a good idea," he told her. "She might be contagious or something."

He's a bad liar, Talia decided. A very bad liar.

She swallowed hard. She felt really hurt.

What was his problem anyway?

"Okay," she said. "Will you call me tomorrow?"

"Sure," he said. "Tomorrow."

Talia hung up the phone, jumped up from her bed, and started to pace back and forth.

What now?

Nervous energy raced through her body. I need to do something, she thought. To occupy my mind. I need to forget about Seth, about Shandel—about everything.

Her eyes landed on her computer.

Why not write a story? A really scary story for the next time the Thrill Club meets.

Horror therapy!

Talia booted up the computer and stared at the empty screen. The cursor flashed impatiently. She sat silently, concentrating as hard as she could. Waiting for inspiration.

Why can't I think?

Talia kept drawing a blank. Every time she tried

to picture a character, all she could see was Shandel lying in the grass.

Staring at the blank screen, at the flashing cursor, Talia lost all track of time.

It was almost a relief when the doorbell rang. Maybe it's Seth, she thought. Maybe his mother had a miraculous recovery.

She checked her hair in the dresser mirror, then hurried downstairs and opened the door.

She gasped.

Two men in dark suits stood on her porch. Both of them were holding up their wallets, which contained police badges. She remembered the shorter one from the night of Shandel's murder.

"Talia Blanton," he said. "I'm Detective Monroe. We spoke briefly the other night. This is my partner, Detective Frazier."

"We need to talk to you," Detective Frazier said in a gentle voice. "Are your parents home?"

"They're at a dinner party," Talia replied. "They should be home in an hour or so."

I wish they were here right now, she thought to herself.

"Can I ask you one question?" Detective Monroe asked quietly.

"Okay," said Talia.

Frazier ran his fingers through his thinning hair.

Why is he staring at me like that? Talia wondered. She avoided his harsh gaze.

"Did you just phone Shandel Carter's mother?" asked Frazier.

"Mrs. Carter? No," Talia replied. "I haven't spoken to her since—since the funeral."

Monroe scratched his head. He seemed puzzled. "Do you want to think about that?" he asked, narrowing his eyes at her. "It's important that you tell us the truth."

"I *am* telling the truth," Talia insisted.

The two detectives exchanged glances. "This is very strange," said Frazier. "Mrs. Carter just called the station to report that you phoned her a short while ago and confessed to murdering her daughter."

chapter 12

Monday at lunch Talia walked carefully through the cafeteria with her tray, searching for a place to sit. Why is everyone staring at me? she wondered. Can't they leave me alone?

Maura and Nessa were huddled together at a table near the window. Talia sighed with relief when she spotted them. Finally, she thought, some familiar faces. People who aren't staring at me like I'm a freak from the circus.

Talia Blanton, the Knife-wielding Maniac.

She didn't know how, but the rumor about the phone call to Mrs. Carter had spread throughout the whole school.

Maura and Nessa, leaning across their trays, talked in hushed voices. They fell silent as soon as they noticed Talia, as though protecting a secret.

"Hi," Talia said a little too loudly. "You guys mind if I sit down?"

"How's it going?" Nessa asked, making room at the table for Talia.

Talia got settled. Maura and Nessa didn't resume their conversation.

"So," asked Talia, "what were you talking about?"

"Homework," Maura replied quickly.

"Boys," said Nessa at the exact same moment.

Talia frowned. They were talking about me, she realized. Everybody's talking about me. I'm the only topic of conversation in the entire school.

When will I get my life back?

"Actually," Nessa confessed, "we were wondering how you were doing. We've been hearing some pretty weird rumors."

"I—I guess I'm okay," murmured Talia even though she'd known that people were watching her and whispering her name all day.

What was she supposed to do? Stand up on the table and announce that she was innocent, that she hadn't murdered Shandel?

Nessa took a sip of her Coke. Talia saw that her eyes were still puffy from crying. "It's been a tough week for everyone," Nessa said softly. "I miss Shandel so much."

Talia stared down at her plate. Her hamburger looked about as appetizing as her notebook. She hadn't eaten anything all day. Her desire for food had simply disappeared.

"I can't understand what's going on," she said.

Her voice broke with emotion. "I think someone's trying to make it look like I—like I—killed Shandel. The police think so too. *They* don't think I did it."

"*No one* thinks you killed her," Nessa assured her.

I wish it were true, Talia thought. But why were all the kids in the lunchroom staring at her?

And why had the police insisted on questioning her for an hour after her parents got home Saturday night?

Talia's attention was drawn back to the conversation.

"Whatever happens, we've got to keep the Thrill Club together," Nessa was saying in a strong voice. "We've got to go on living normal lives. I think that's what Shandel would have wanted."

A normal life?

The phrase stuck in Talia's mind. Will I ever have a normal life again? Can any of us?

Will I ever sit in this cafeteria again and not feel like everyone's studying me, wondering if I cut my friend's throat?

Talia glanced up, suddenly aware of Maura's green eyes watching her closely. Maura hadn't said a word since Talia sat down.

She thinks I did it, Talia realized. Maura really thinks I'm a monster.

I can't stand it, she thought. I've got to get out of here. She jumped up abruptly, leaving her food untouched on the table.

Maura and Nessa stared at her in bewilderment.

"I—I'll see you later, okay?" Talia said.

The drone of lunchtime conversation seemed to stop dead the moment Talia stood up. As she hurried toward the door, she had the feeling that every eye in the room was on her.

I've got to get out of here, Talia thought desperately. *Got to get out!*

Talia felt better the moment she escaped from the cafeteria. It was so stuffy in there. *So much cooler and quieter here in the deserted hallway. I can breathe again.*

She almost wished she could find an empty classroom, curl up in the corner, and sleep the day away.

Then I could wake up and find out that this is all a bad dream. Just a scary story. Shandel will laugh when she reads it.

She chuckled grimly. *Nice try, Talia.* She knew it was no dream.

Shandel will never laugh at anything again.

She passed the music room. The Shadyside High chorus was practicing. Talia glanced through the window. The singers stood in three neat rows, holding sheet music in their hands. Their voices mingled in close harmony.

The music was soothing somehow. Talia began to feel a little better.

The sound of singing followed her down the hallway until she turned the corner leading to the gym. Just as she was passing the boys' locker room, Rudy stepped out the door and into the hall.

He stared at her in surprise. He wore blue bike

shorts and a sleeveless T-shirt, and had a leather weightlifting belt wrapped tightly around his waist.

"Talia," he said, "I was just thinking about you."

Talia couldn't help smiling. Such a soothing voice. *I can trust Rudy. He's one of the nicest people I know.*

Approaching footsteps echoed down the corridor. Rudy glanced nervously down the empty hallway. He touched Talia's arm. "Let's go in the gym," he told her. "We can talk."

Rudy pushed open the door, and Talia followed him into the darkened gym. It felt strange to be standing alone in the dim, empty space with Rudy. *Like we're hiding from the world,* Talia thought to herself.

"What's up?" she asked.

Rudy shyly lowered his eyes to the floor. "I—I've heard the crazy rumors about you, Talia," he said softly. "I just want you to know I don't believe them."

"Thanks, Rudy," she said, sighing. "I think this has been the worst week of my life. Sometimes I think I'm going crazy."

"It'll just take time," he said softly. "And listen—if there's anything I can do . . ." His voice trailed off.

Oh, Rudy, Talia thought. *I could kiss you for that.* She smiled at him in the darkness. "Thank you," she whispered.

Seth's face flashed across her mind. Talia still felt angry at him for standing her up on Saturday and not calling her on Sunday.

Seth had let her down when she needed him most.

And here was Rudy, so kind and caring.

Yes. Caring.

He really cares about me, she thought.

The next thing she knew, her arms were around his neck, her lips pressing softly against his.

Rudy's lips pressed back.

Talia closed her eyes, surrendering to the moment.

Behind them, the gym door swung open with a creak.

Someone gasped.

Talia and Rudy pulled away from each other, whirling toward the sound.

Too late.

The door had already swung shut.

"Who—who saw us?" Talia stammered.

chapter 13

Talia raced for the door. Rudy followed close behind.

Out in the hall, she turned in both directions. No one in sight.

She heard footsteps vanishing around the corner.

"Oh, well," said Rudy. "No sense chasing after him."

"Or her," Talia added.

In the light, Talia could see that he was blushing.

"I'm sorry," she told him. "I hope that wasn't Maura. She'd be furious."

"It might have been Seth," he reminded her. "Then you'd be the one in trouble."

"I know," said Talia. "Things with Seth and me haven't been going that great as it is."

Rudy didn't respond. He ran his fingers through

his short brown hair and stared down the long, empty corridor.

Talia didn't know what had possessed her to kiss Rudy so impulsively. She really liked him, but only as a friend.

"Maybe it was a teacher," Rudy suggested. "Or someone who doesn't even know us."

"Maybe," Talia agreed, wishing she could believe it was true. She felt guilty. If Seth had been treating her better, she would never have kissed Rudy.

"Oh, well." Rudy shrugged. "It was just one kiss. What's the big deal?"

Thursday morning Talia stared miserably at her waffles. The waffles stared back, floating in a sticky pool of syrup. The most important meal of the day.

"Mom," she groaned. "I really can't eat this morning."

"Honey—" Her mother's voice was soft but firm. "You have to try. You've hardly eaten anything for days. I know you're upset. But you've really got to start eating again."

"I'm sorry, Mom. I'm just not hungry." Talia knew she was being stubborn, but she couldn't help it. Her appetite had disappeared along with her normal life.

For once her mother didn't argue. "Okay," she said, forcing a smile. "Forget the waffles. Get your books. I'll drive you to school."

Talia was silent in the car, nervously smoothing the fabric of her dress. All week long she'd worn jeans to school. But that morning she'd forced herself to dress up. She wore a tight blue tank dress, with black high-heeled sandals. If people were going to stare at her, she might as well give them something to stare at.

Her mother hummed along with a song on the radio, sneaking quick glances at Talia from the corner of her eye. At a red light, Mrs. Blanton turned to Talia.

"Honey," she said, "talk to me. Sometimes it helps."

Talia didn't know what to say. Both of her parents had been wonderful over the past couple of weeks, so understanding and supportive. And of course her mother's legal knowledge was a big help. But Talia just didn't feel like having a heart-to-heart talk this morning.

I can't take any more questions, she thought. Not even from my mother. I just want to be left alone.

"Everything's fine," Talia said defensively.

Her mother nodded, frowning. "And how's Seth?" she asked. "He hasn't been around for a week."

"He's been busy," Talia explained. "He's got a lot of chores at home."

"I see," said Mrs. Blanton. "Well, why not invite him over for dinner tonight?"

"Okay," Talia said. "I'll see what he says."

Fat chance, she thought to herself. Seth has hardly said two words to me all week.

They pulled into the Shadyside High parking lot.

Talia stepped out of the car. A familiar feeling of dread came over her as she approached the school.

I don't want to be here, she thought. I can't take another day of everyone staring at me.

She took a deep breath and gathered her courage. Forcing her shoulders back erect, she entered the building, forcing a smile on her face. Be strong, she told herself.

She shifted her backpack on her shoulders and walked slowly down the hall to her locker. Maybe I *will* invite Seth over for dinner, she thought. We need to talk. After kissing Rudy in the gym, Talia realized that Seth was still the one she wanted.

Seth is my boyfriend, she told herself.

Rudy is just my friend.

Seth and I have got to start talking again. I miss his smile. The way we used to talk for hours on the telephone. I miss holding hands at the movies.

I miss him.

She took her books out of her locker and decided to search for Seth, to see if she could persuade him to accept her mother's invitation.

Walking through the hall, she realized that only a couple of kids stared at her as she passed. The others went on with their business, talking and laughing among themselves, hardly even noticing her.

Wow, she thought with relief. Maybe things are getting back to normal. Maybe I'll be okay.

Walking past the library, she heard a familiar laugh and turned toward the sound. She saw Nessa standing in front of her locker in a pair of skin-tight jeans, laughing at something a tall, thin boy had told her. The boy had his back to Talia.

Nessa threw back her head and laughed again, tossing her soft, dark hair. She ran her hand down the length of the boy's arm, letting her long fingers trail softly over his wrist. Her laughter rang out in the hallway, a bright, happy sound.

Nessa's such a flirt, Talia thought with a smile. Last week it was the wrestler. The week before that it was the guy from the junior college. And this week?

As if responding to Talia's unspoken question, the boy of the week turned around.

Talia's mouth dropped open. Her books fell right out of her hand.

Seth.

How could he?

And how could Nessa? I thought she was my friend.

Talia picked up her books and walked as calmly as she could over to Nessa's locker. She put her hand on Seth's shoulder and looked Nessa straight in the eye.

"What's up?" she demanded, trying to sound casual. "You two seem awfully friendly."

Seth blushed. Nessa's mouth dropped open in surprise.

"B-but, Talia," she finally stammered. "You said it was okay. You told me last night you were breaking up with Seth."

"Me?" Talia gasped. "I told you what?"

"On the phone," Nessa insisted. "You told me I

should go out with Seth. You said it was okay. Did you suddenly forget, Talia? We talked for nearly an hour."

Talia felt dizzy. She wondered if she was going to faint.

"Nessa," she managed to choke out. "I didn't call you last night. We didn't talk on the phone. We didn't!"

chapter 14

"Talia—how can you lie like that?" Nessa demanded. "I'm not crazy. We talked last night. Right after dinner."

"I'm not crazy either!" Talia shouted shrilly. "I never talked to you, Nessa."

Nessa bit her lip, eyeing Talia angrily. "You said you were breaking up with Seth, and that it was all right if I asked him out. Maura was over at my house. She was as shocked as I was."

Seth pulled out from under Talia's arm. "What's going on here, Talia? What's the story?"

"No, I never said it," Talia insisted to Nessa. "Why are you telling lies about me?"

"I'm not lying," Nessa muttered. "Why would I?"

Talia turned to Seth. "You have to believe me."

"I don't know what to believe," Seth declared.

Talia searched their faces. They're my friends, she thought. They don't want to hurt me.

Or do they?

Something is wrong here. Something is terribly wrong. First the call to Shandel's mother, and now this.

Who's making these calls?

It has to be someone who can sound just like me. Someone who sounds so much like me that even Nessa was fooled?

Am I going crazy? Or is someone trying to ruin my life?

Will somebody please tell me what's going on?

Talia's parents left at seven for the Neighborhood Improvement Association meeting. Her father was an architect and had lots of ideas he was eager to share for sprucing up Shadyside's parks and municipal buildings.

Talia locked the door behind them and sat down at the kitchen table. Now that her brother was away at college, she often found herself home alone at night when her parents were working late or attending meetings for their numerous organizations.

It was easier for her to do homework without Dave around to tease her or blast his heavy-metal music, but it was also a lot less fun.

Oh, well, she thought, opening her math book and staring at the homework problems. Next year I'll be away at college myself. Then the house will be empty.

I have to concentrate, she told herself. I have to start doing my schoolwork. Since the murder, she'd fallen behind in her classes.

Maybe I should call Seth, she thought. Ask him for some pointers. He's the math genius, after all.

Maybe that would be a good excuse to talk to him. Talia didn't even know if they were going out anymore. Four days had passed since she'd seen him at his locker. He didn't even know she'd been accepted to UC Berkeley.

No, she decided. I can't call him now. I have to do these math problems by myself.

She figured out the first cquation. It felt good, likc solving a puzzle. She started in on the second one.

Maybe she could ace the next test. Win back Mr. Hanson's trust. That would be a start.

She had nearly finished the second equation, when the doorbell rang.

Oh, no, she thought. What now?

Her heart pounded in her chest as she stood up and walked toward the door. The sound of the bell filled her with dread these days.

Would it be the police? Back to ask more questions about Shandel?

Would it be more bad news?

She stopped in front of the door. Silence.

Then three sharp knocks came.

"Who is it?" she called.

No reply.

She took a deep breath and pulled open the door.

And uttered a shriek of horror when she saw the hideous face move close to hers.

"Talia . . ." it croaked. *"Talia . . ."*

"No!" she screamed. "No—don't! Please!"

chapter 15

Seth pulled off the hideous mask and grinned at Talia.

"Gotcha!" he cried, and burst out laughing.

For a few seconds Talia couldn't speak. She just stared at him in angry disbelief.

"Seth—you creep!" she finally managed to choke out. "How could you?"

"Sorry," he said, still laughing. "I thought you'd know it was me. I didn't know you'd have a cow! I thought you'd just laugh and tell me to come in."

He held up the mask. Carved wood, decorated with garish slashes of orange and green. The mouth was a huge white *O,* frozen in a scream. The eyes were angry slits.

"Isn't this awesome?" he asked. "It's an aboriginal mask from New Guinea. My father collected a whole bunch of great tribal artifacts on his last visit. I thought maybe I'd wear it to the Thrill Club meeting at Rudy's tomorrow night."

Talia studied the mask as she led him into the living room. As ferocious as it was, there was also something amusing about it. It was so exaggerated, like a Halloween mask.

"I'm sorry I went bonkers," she told Seth. "I guess I'm just not in a laughing mood these days." She forced herself to smile. "But I really am happy to see you."

"Me too." Seth set the mask down on the coffee table and hugged her. Talia didn't want to let go. "I don't want to lose you," he told her.

"I was worried," she whispered. "I thought you were going to break up with me."

"No way. I wasn't going to break up with you," he insisted. "I thought you were going to break up with me."

Talia hugged him tighter. "I'm sorry, Seth. Things have just been so confusing lately. So many crazy things have happened. Sometimes I don't know if I'm losing my mind or what."

"We'll be okay," he told her, brushing the hair away from her eyes.

Talia went into the kitchen to get Seth a Coke. She felt happier than she had in a long time. She returned to the living room, handed Seth the can, and sat down beside him on the couch.

The mask leered at her from the coffee table.

It really is the ugliest thing I've ever seen, she thought.

"So what's up?" Seth asked cheerfully. He took a

sip from his Coke. "It feels like a hundred years since we've really had a good talk."

Oh, well, she thought. I guess I better tell him now. No sense putting it off. Talia took a deep breath. "I know there hasn't been much good news lately," she began. "But guess what I got in the mail today?"

"What?"

"My acceptance to UC Berkeley! Isn't that great?"

Seth fumbled for an answer. Talia could sense his disappointment.

Ever since January, when they'd submitted their applications to colleges, he'd been trying to persuade her to stay in the area, maybe go to the state university with him.

"California's awfully far away," he said glumly.

"Not that far," Talia replied. But she knew better. California seemed like another world. A place of sunshine and happiness. Where she could start a new life, put the past behind her.

"Besides," she reminded him, "I'll be home for vacations. And we can write. It'll be okay."

"I don't know," Seth said doubtfully. "I don't think I like this."

Talia was touched by his sadness. He really does care about me, she thought. Things have been so confusing. I can't believe I almost let him slip away again.

Seth reached into his jacket pocket and pulled out a folded sheaf of papers. "By the way," he said. "I almost forgot. I brought something for you."

Talia took the papers from his hand.

"It's a horror story," he continued. "I know you've still got writer's block, so I wrote this for you. To read at tomorrow night's meeting."

"What?" Talia cried, surprised.

"What's the matter?" Seth asked casually.

"Do you really think we should do another scary story?" Talia replied thoughtfully.

"Why not?" Seth asked. "I'm not superstitious—are you? Besides, what could happen?"

chapter 16

Rudy glanced up at the ceiling of his parents' basement rec room. Those water pipes up there will be perfect, he thought. The Thrill Club will love this!

This will be the most awesome prank of the year!

Rudy heard footsteps and turned toward the sound. His eight-year-old brother Pete was standing at the foot of the basement stairs, peering at Rudy through his thick glasses.

"Hey," called Pete. "What are you doing with that big rope?"

Rudy stepped onto a folding chair and tossed one end of the rope over the exposed pipe. He tied a knot in the rope and stepped down, admiring his handiwork.

This is going to be so cool! I can't wait to see their faces.

"Hey, Pete—look," he told his brother excitedly. "You know the ventriloquist dummy Dad picked up at that garage sale? The one with the bow tie and all those freckles? The one that's almost as big as you are?"

Pete nodded. He couldn't take his eyes off the dangling rope.

"Well," Rudy continued, "the Thrill Club is coming over for tonight's meeting. When they get here, I'm going to have the room real dark, so it's hard to see. And that dummy's going to be hanging from that overhead pipe. With a noose tied around his neck."

Pete's eyes widened.

"Pretty funny," Pete said. He would never allow himself to show any real enthusiasm for any trick of Rudy's. Too many of Rudy's tricks were played on him!

Pete put both hands around his own throat and pretended to choke. "I'm hanging! I'm hanging!" he cried.

Rudy laughed. His little brother always cracked him up.

"Everyone will come down into the dark and bump into the dummy hanging from the ceiling," Rudy said gleefully. "They'll freak. They really will."

"Can I watch?" Pete asked eagerly.

"Sure," said Rudy. "You can hide in the closet. It'll be a riot."

"Great." Pete stared up at the rope.

"Don't tell Mom and Dad," Rudy warned.

"No problem," Pete replied. He scampered back up the steps, leaving Rudy alone with his project.

Rudy opened the closet and pulled out the dummy. It was so real looking, Rudy almost felt as if they could have a conversation.

"Hey, pal," he said, reaching out to shake the dummy's wooden hand. "How've you been? Enjoying your stay in the closet? Dark enough for you in there?"

The dummy didn't answer. He just stared at Rudy with his glassy eyes and painted-on smile.

All right, thought Rudy. Be that way.

"For the crime of rudeness," he told the dummy, "I sentence you to hung by the neck until you die."

The dummy didn't seem to mind. He just sat there in his little plaid coat and bow tie, grinning his eternal grin.

Rudy set the dummy on the couch.

"Your honor," he said, addressing an imaginary judge, "the defendant shows no remorse."

Rudy climbed back up on the folding chair, grabbed the loose end of the rope, and began fashioning it into a noose. He had been a Scout, and earned a merit badge for knot-tying.

Now his training came in handy. When he was done, the noose dangled ominously from the pipe, waiting for a victim.

This is going to be way cool! Rudy thought again.

He picked up the dummy and carried him over to the noose. He tried to slip the rope over the wooden head, but it wouldn't fit.

Darn. I made it too small.

He set the dummy down and climbed back up on the chair. Carefully, he retied the noose. This time the opening was large enough.

On an impulse, out of curiosity, Rudy slipped it over his own head. The rope hung loosely around his neck.

"See?" he called to the dummy down below. "There's nothing to it."

The dummy grinned up at Rudy in silent agreement.

Balancing on the folding chair, Rudy reached up to remove the noose.

"Hey—"

He struggled a bit and accidentally pulled on the knot.

The noose tightened.

"Hey—"

Frightened, Rudy really started to lose his balance now.

"Hey—"

The rope tightened more, cutting deep into his throat.

"Pete?" he choked. "Pete? Can you hear me?"

Silence.

"Pete?"

The only sound was the creaking of the pipe over his head.

"Help! Somebody! I—can't—breathe!"

Clawing at the rope, he kicked back.

He saw the dummy grinning up at him. A ghoulish, gleeful grin.

And then Rudy felt the chair move as it fell out from under him.

"Aaaaaaack!"

Rudy's final gasping cry—as he swung over the floor, tearing helplessly at the noose until everything went black.

chapter 17

"Excellent!" exclaimed Talia.

Seth beamed at the compliment.

"That's an excellent horror story!" Talia repeated, shaking her head in admiration. "Really outstanding."

Seth continued to grin, pleased by her reaction. "I know I'm not as good a writer as you, but I'm getting better."

Talia stared at the horrible mask on the coffee table. "The story is great, but I feel uncomfortable," she confessed.

"About what?" Seth demanded.

"I really don't want to read a story to the Thrill Club using Rudy's name. You know—after what happened to Shandel."

"But, Talia—"

"Can't we just change the name? Use Rick instead of Rudy, or something like that?" Talia suggested.

"Why?" asked Seth. He seemed surprised by her suggestion.

"Why!" Talia was flabbergasted. "Because it will just make everyone think of Shandel. Most of them already suspect that I killed her," she added glumly.

Seth's mouth curled into a thoughtful smile. "That's why I think we should keep Rudy's name in it," Seth said. "If you read this story tomorrow night, people will understand that you're innocent."

Talia didn't follow his reasoning. Seth was smart, but his mind worked in strange ways.

"How?" she demanded. "How could reading a story about Rudy accidentally hanging himself prove anything about what happened to Shandel?"

"Simple," declared Seth. "By reading another story with a real name in it, you'll prove to everyone that you have nothing to hide. That you don't have a guilty conscience. That everything is the same as always."

Talia nodded thoughtfully. What Seth said made a certain kind of sense. "There's only one problem," she said.

Seth raised his eyebrows. "What's that?"

"Rudy will hate it," Talia said. "He'll think I'm out to get him or something."

Seth shook his head. "No way. You know Rudy has a great sense of humor. Besides, it'll ruin the story if you change the name. Everyone knows that

Rudy is the guy with the noose. He rigs that noose up in his rec room every single time we hold the meeting at his house. He'll think the story is a riot. Really, Talia."

Talia didn't know what to think. She wanted to read the story. But the final picture was just so gross. Rudy dangling, grasping at the noose, choking for air. The dummy grinning up at him.

Should I read it or not? she asked herself.

I have until tomorrow night to decide.

After school the next afternoon Talia stared into the darkness of her locker. I'm forgetting something, she thought. What is it that I'm supposed to bring home?

A hand fell on her shoulder—and she jumped.

Rudy pulled his hand away. "Whoa. Sorry." He seemed startled by her reaction. "I didn't mean to scare you. I just wanted to say hello."

Talia felt foolish. She smiled sheepishly. "It's okay, Rudy. I'm so stressed out these days, I jump at anything."

Rudy nodded sympathetically.

He's so cute, Talia thought, blushing at the memory of their kiss. Neither of them had mentioned it in the days since it happened.

We're just friends, she reminded herself. It will have to stay that way.

"Anyway," said Rudy, "I just wanted to make sure you were coming to the Thrill Club meeting at my house tonight. It wouldn't be the same without you."

"Of course I'm coming!" Talia exclaimed. "I wouldn't miss it for anything." She lowered her voice. "Do you need any help? Can I bring anything? Do anything? Are you going to put up any creepy decorations?"

"Oh, yeah," Rudy said with a wink, "I have something scary planned."

He's putting up his noose again, Talia told herself.

"If you want, I could come over early and help you set everything up," she offered.

"Really?" Rudy seemed excited. "Thanks. I'm dying to hear your new story."

Talia's heart sank. The image of Rudy's head in a tightening noose flashed before her eyes. Do I really want to read that story?

"I'm not sure about this new story," Talia said truthfully. "I may not read it at all."

"You have to," Rudy insisted. "Your stories are the best part of our meetings."

"Well," said Talia reluctantly, "maybe I'll read it to you first and see what you think." She touched Rudy softly on the arm. "What time should I come over?"

"How about six?" suggested Rudy. "That should give us enough time to put up the decorations and read the story."

"Great." Talia grinned. "See you tonight."

Spring had finally arrived. The afternoon was bright and sunny. The air smelled sweet and fresh.

Daffodils bloomed. Fresh leaves were beginning to unfurl on the trees.

It's so beautiful, Talia thought, wandering through Shadyside Park after school. A fresh start. Maybe everything will be all right after all.

She heard footsteps rushing behind her and spun around to see who it was.

Maura came jogging up the path. She stopped when she caught up with Talia. She was breathing hard, her cheeks ruddy from the exercise.

"Talia," she gasped, "where did you ever learn to walk so fast? I've been chasing you for three blocks."

"Why were you chasing me?" Talia asked suspiciously. "Is something wrong?"

"Not really." Maura caught her breath and smiled. "I just wanted to talk to you about . . . something."

Rudy, Talia thought. She must have been the one who saw Rudy and me kissing in the gym. Talia braced herself.

"Talk to me?" she asked casually. "About what?"

"Talia," Maura began, "I know we're not the best of friends. And I know it's really none of my business, but I'm worried about Seth."

"About Seth?" Talia bristled. Maura has no right to poke her nose into my relationship with Seth. She spoke sharply. "What about Seth, Maura?"

Maura hesitated. "He—uh—well, I think he's cracking up, Talia. I'm so worried about him. I think he's totally losing it!"

chapter 18

"Maura—what are you *talking* about?" Talia demanded shrilly.

Maura took a deep breath. "Well—from my bedroom window, I can see into his room. All he does is pace. At night. Back and forth. Sometimes all night long. He seems to be terribly stoked about something."

Talia gaped at her. "He paces all night?"

Maura nodded. "Yeah. And he does weird things. He waves his arms around like he's talking to himself. And when he's not pacing, he sits at his desk going through papers and tapes. I guess they must be his father's. It's like he's obsessed or something."

"Wow," Talia murmured.

Maura frowned. "I care about Seth, Talia. I just

thought you should know about him. About how strange he's acting."

Talia could picture it. Poor Seth. Haunted by the death of his father. Trying to understand a terrible tragedy.

But Maura had no right to intrude on his private grief. Even if she was his next-door neighbor and could see into his bedroom window.

"Is that all?" Talia snapped. "You chased me for three blocks to tell me that you've been spying on my boyfriend? Maybe you should get a life, Maura. Maybe you should just pull down your shades and leave Seth alone."

The color returned to Maura's cheeks. She sounded really hurt. "You don't understand, Talia. I just wanted you to know so you could help him. He's your boyfriend. I accept that. It's just that I still care about him as a friend."

Talia could feel herself losing control. "Oh, I understand," she said shrilly. "I understand perfectly. You're spying on my boyfriend and following me around. Maybe you should mind your own business for a change."

"I'm sorry you feel that way," Maura replied, staring unhappily at the ground. She ran her fingers through her red hair. "I was only trying to help." She looked up, frowning at Talia. "Maybe we should just cancel the meeting tonight. Maybe we've had enough thrills for a while. I think we could all use a rest."

"It's too late to cancel it," Talia said quickly. "Which reminds me. I've got to run, Maura. I promised Rudy I'd get to his house early to help him get ready."

"What?" Maura seemed shocked. *"You're* going early to Rudy's?"

Whoops, thought Talia. Maybe I shouldn't have mentioned that. Well, too bad for Maura. If she can stay home and spy on Seth, then I can help Rudy prepare for the meeting.

Talia turned and walked away. She could feel Maura's eyes on her, burning into her back.

Nessa couldn't wait to get to the Thrill Club meeting at Rudy's. I need to do something fun, she told herself. Life has been so grim lately. All I do is sit around and brood about Shandel.

Walking briskly through the warm evening air, the sun just dipping behind the trees, she tried to predict what Rudy would have hanging from the noose on his ceiling.

He had hinted to her earlier that that night's prop would be his best ever—though Nessa couldn't believe that anything could outdo the lifelike mannequin he'd used for the last meeting.

She smiled to herself, remembering the shock of it: a man in a business suit, swaying back forth above the floor, a look of pure shock frozen on his plastic face.

It was so gross. They all made jokes about it the whole evening.

Oh, well, she thought. Better not underestimate Rudy. He's got a really great imagination.

When Nessa arrived at Rudy's, she found Maura

and Seth standing on the front porch, puzzled expressions on their faces.

"Hey—what's up?" Nessa greeted them eagerly. "Did you ring the bell?"

Seth nodded. He was wearing his black jeans and camouflage shirt—his usual outfit. He reached up and scratched his head. "Three times," he replied. "And Rudy still hasn't answered."

"What's his problem!" Maura said huffily. "He knows we're coming."

"Where are his parents?" Nessa asked.

"Rudy told me today they were going to take Pete to a Cub Scout meeting," said Maura. She pressed her finger against the doorbell and held it there for a long time. "Rudy will have to hear this."

They waited another minute or so. Nessa pressed her face against the door to peer inside. Maybe this is part of the joke, she suddenly realized.

"The door's open," she pointed out after jiggling the handle. "Why don't we let ourselves in?"

"Let's give him another minute or two," Seth suggested. "It doesn't seem right to barge into someone's house."

They stood impatiently on the porch, trading nervous smiles in the warm spring evening. A blue car drove slowly past the house, country music blasting from its open windows. They watched it vanish around the corner.

Seth chewed anxiously on his fingernails. "I hope Talia gets here soon."

"She's supposed to be here already," Maura

informed them in a peevish voice. "She told me she was coming over early to help Rudy decorate. I'm sure they're down there. I can't understand why they're making us wait like this."

Nessa tried to conceal her surprise. What was Talia doing alone in the basement with Rudy, while Maura waited outside? It seemed a bit suspicious, to say the least.

Especially the way Talia had been acting lately, calling her to say she wanted to break up with Seth, then denying it had ever happened.

Nessa reached for the door. "What are we waiting for?" she demanded. "Let's go down there and see what's keeping them."

Seth held the door open so the girls could enter first. Nessa blinked to get used to the darkness of the house.

A strange silence hung in the air as they passed through the kitchen on their way to the cellar door. They paused at the top of the stairs.

"Rudy!" Maura called out. "Talia! Are you down there?"

No reply.

Maura turned to Nessa with a confused expression on her face. "I can't understand it," she said. "They were supposed to be here."

Nessa bit her lip and tried to think. "Maybe they went to the store or something," she speculated.

"We're here," Seth said decisively. "We might as well check out the basement."

They made their way downstairs single file, with

Nessa bringing up the rear. The wooden steps creaked beneath their weight. At the bottom of the stairs they turned right to enter the rec room.

Nessa heard the others gasp before she saw the body.

Then she saw Rudy.

Hanging from the overhead pipes, a clean white rope knotted tightly around his neck.

His face seemed enormous above the noose, purple and twisted with horror.

Maura brought her hands to her mouth to stifle a cry. She wobbled a little, as if she might faint.

Sensing her anguish, Nessa reached out and grabbed her by the arm.

"He hanged himself," Seth murmured, his eyes riveted on the gruesome sight.

Nessa felt her stomach quiver.

"Ohhhhh," Maura moaned.

Then, without warning, Nessa began to laugh.

High, giddy laughter.

She couldn't stop.

chapter

19

Nessa laughed so hard, her stomach began to hurt.

Seth and Maura gaped at her in shock. "Nessa—what's *wrong* with you?" Maura cried.

Nessa struggled to catch her breath. She ignored Maura's question. "Okay, Rudy," she sputtered. "You can come down now."

A heavy silence fell over the room. The only sound was the creaking of the ceiling pipes.

Seth's mouth dropped open, but no sound came out. Maura's eyes narrowed at Nessa.

"Nessa—stop laughing!" Maura choked out.

"Don't you see? It's a joke!" Nessa cried, tears of laughter running down her pale cheeks. "Rudy told me he was cooking up something extra-special for tonight's meeting."

"Nessa—no—" Maura whispered.

Rudy swayed over the carpet, his face purple in the fluorescent light.

"Come down, Rudy!" Nessa cried. "You fooled us. Come down now."

She turned to Maura and Seth. "It's a joke, guys. Don't you see?"

"Nessa—please. It—it's no joke," Maura stammered.

Seth swallowed hard, his eyes on the swaying body.

Nessa's stomach tightened with fear. "Yes, it is," she insisted. "It's a joke. It *has* to be."

She took a step toward the body. "Rudy—how did you get your face so purple?" she cried. "How did you do it, Rudy? Tell us!"

Then she turned back to her two horrified friends. "It's a joke. I'm telling you—it's a joke!" she insisted, suddenly shrill and uncertain.

Maura didn't reply. She walked unsteadily over to the body. She grabbed hold of Rudy's arm and pulled it away from his body.

The expression on Rudy's distorted face didn't change. Maura let go of the arm. It dropped limply, lifelessly, back to his side.

"It's no joke," Maura repeated softly, gazing up at her boyfriend's purple face. "Oh, Rudy," she whimpered. "Who did this to you?" As though her legs couldn't hold her up, Maura dropped slowly to her knees and hid her face in her hands.

Nessa felt as if she couldn't breathe. The shriek she made seemed to come from somewhere outside of herself. "He's dead!" she heard herself screaming. "Rudy's dead! What is happening to us?"

Nessa's knees buckled and she started to sway. Seth caught her in his arms. Holding on tightly to his shoulders, Nessa began to cry as well.

The basement room echoed with the wailing of their grief. Seth patted Nessa softly on the back, trying to comfort her.

"Someone call the police," Maura whispered through her tears. "We've got to get help."

Seth walked Nessa slowly over to the couch and lowered her to the cushion. "Where's the phone?" he asked, glancing quickly around the room.

"Upstairs," Maura sobbed, still kneeling by Rudy's body. "Please—get help."

Seth touched his hand to Nessa's cheek. Nessa couldn't stop crying. She felt hot tears running down her face.

"Just close your eyes and sit tight," Seth instructed her. "I'm going to run upstairs and call the police. I'll be back in a minute."

Nessa watched through her tear-blurred eyes as Seth took two quick steps toward the stairs, then froze. His eyes widened. He yelped in surprise.

"Talia!"

Nessa gasped as Talia stumbled out of the shadows beneath the stairwell. Her blond hair hung across her face in a wild tangle.

She seemed dazed, unaware of her surroundings. Her eyes were unfocused as she moved unsteadily into the light with a strange, vacant smile on her face. She held her hands awkwardly in front of her, the fingers bent like claws.

"Talia!" Seth cried. "We thought—" He broke off in midsentence, staring at her hands.

"Your hands," he gasped. "What's the matter with your hands? They're all red and cut. Are those—*rope* burns?"

chapter

20

The nurse poked her head into the clean white room. "Talia," she said in a friendly voice, "you have a visitor."

Talia sat up in bed, smoothing the front of her wrinkled cotton nightgown. She hurriedly tried to fix her hair, but then abandoned the effort.

What's the point? she thought. After what I've done, who cares what my hair looks like? Why would anyone ever want to see me again?

She stared blankly at her bandaged hands. She didn't look up until she heard the voice.

"Talia?" Seth stood shyly in the doorway, watching her with his gentle eyes. "It's me."

Talia couldn't help but smile. It was so good to see him again.

I feel as if I've been in this hospital for months.

ing quickly through the rows of cars in the parking lot. A red-haired girl stepped out from behind a station wagon to greet him.

Oh, no! Talia thought, squinting to see better. It can't be!

Maura.

Seth and Maura.

Maura and Seth.

Talia shook her head, as if trying to shake away the scene below her window.

But when she peered down again, the two of them remained.

Maura and Seth stood close together in the middle of the parking lot. They spoke for a short time, and then Maura put her arm around Seth's shoulder.

They walked together to Seth's car, walked together like a couple.

The couple they used to be.

Talia staggered away from the window, stunned by the betrayal. So Maura wanted Seth back all along, she thought bitterly.

I should have known. I should have seen that Maura wanted him back.

Then, a chilling thought made Talia drop back onto her bed. How badly did Maura want Seth back? How much did she want me out of the way?

Enough to kill for him—and make it look as if it were me?

chapter 21

Later that night, long past midnight, Talia struggled to keep her eyes open. She wanted to finish the book she was reading before going to sleep.

Talia had read six books since entering the hospital. Reading was the only thing that kept her sane, the only activity that reminded her of the life she had had.

As she read, the letters began to blur on the page, mixing in strange nonsense patterns. She blinked her eyes again and again, until the letters finally stopped swirling.

There, she thought. That's better.

Hearing footsteps in the hall, she glanced up. Usually the hospital was silent as a morgue late at night.

The footsteps stopped outside her door.

She heard whispers.

A creak of the door.

Then the sound of her own muffled cry. "Hey—"

Two teenagers stepped into Talia's room. A white boy and an African American girl. Both were dressed in white hospital gowns. They padded softly across the floor until they were standing right next to her bed.

They grinned at her, strange, leering grins.

"Wh-what do you want?" Talia stammered, closing her book and raising herself on the pillow.

They didn't reply. Their grins grew wider.

Talia could hear their breathing, more like groaning.

"Are you patients here?" Talia asked, feeling cold fear run down her back.

They stared at her, breathing hard. The boy giggled, a high-pitched, childish giggle.

"Are you in the wrong room?" Talia asked.

The boy giggled again.

The girl reached out and touched Talia's hair.

"Please—" Talia murmured. "Can you go back to your own rooms? Do you need help?"

The girl petted Talia's hair as if petting a dog. Gently at first, then harder.

"Stop—please!" Talia insisted, feeling another shudder of fear. "Please—"

The boy let out another childish giggle. "Want to play? Want to play with us?" He brought his face close to hers.

"No—" Talia said.

"We can play with your hair," the girl said in a

surprisingly husky voice. She grabbed a strand of Talia's hair and held on.

"Let go!" Talia cried, trying to pull free.

The girl grasped the hair tighter.

"Play with her hair. Play with her hair!" the boy chanted, his shoulders bouncing up and down.

"Nice hair," the girl said, her grin widening. "Nice hair."

"Please—" Talia begged, overcome with fear. "Please—"

She stared up at them, at their wild, unblinking eyes, at their wide grins.

And suddenly recognized them.

Rudy and Shandel.

"You—you're here!" Talia cried as they moved in to attack her.

chapter 22

"Come away! Come away from there!" a harsh voice rasped.

Talia watched as strong hands pulled Rudy and Shandel away.

They didn't struggle. Two young male attendants led them to the door.

"Arnold—Mayrose—did you get confused?" one of the attendants asked gently. "Did you go to the wrong room?"

Shivering, her chest still heaving with fear, Talia shut her eyes and listened until their voices disappeared down the hall.

She could still feel the girl gripping her hair, still see the boy's leering grin.

Arnold? Mayrose?

"Ohhhh." Talia let out a low moan. They weren't

Rudy and Shandel. Of *course* they weren't Rudy and Shandel. They were just two patients who had wandered into the wrong room.

Talia wrapped her arms around her chest, held herself tightly.

What is wrong with me?

What is wrong?

Seth chewed his pencil and studied the math problem. He scribbled some numbers on a sheet of scratch paper, then shook his head.

No, he thought. That can't be right.

Think, he urged himself. Concentrate.

The phone rang. A piercing noise, like an alarm going off. His concentration shattered like a pane of glass. Angrily, he reached for phone.

"Hello?"

It was Talia. Calling from home. She had just been released from the hospital.

"Seth?" She sounded breathless, upset about something. "What are you doing?"

"Right now?" he asked.

"Yes," she replied. "This very minute."

Seth cast a mournful glance at his math homework. "Nothing," he lied. "At least nothing important."

"Can you come over?" she asked. "I really need to talk to you."

"You can talk to me now," he told her.

"I need to *see* you," she insisted. "It's really important."

"Okay," he said, and sighed. Talia could be so demanding sometimes. Especially lately. "When should I come over?"

"Now," she said. "As soon as possible."

He nodded wearily. "I'll be right there."

A short while later Seth parked in front of Talia's house and walked up the steps to the front door. He rang the bell. This had better be important, he thought.

Talia opened the door without a word of greeting. She grabbed him by the arm and led him into the den. She seemed agitated. Her blue eyes glittered with a mysterious light.

Talia sat down on the couch. She patted the cushion beside her.

"Sit down," she said. "Don't be afraid."

Afraid, thought Seth. Do I seem afraid? He settled onto the couch, reaching for her hand.

"I could never be frightened of you," he said soothingly. "I know you'd never hurt anyone."

"You're probably the only one left," she muttered unhappily. "Everyone else thinks I'm some kind of psycho. They want to lock me up, Seth."

"That's not true," Seth lied to her. "You just have to be patient. Right now everyone's upset and confused. They don't know what to believe. There's a killer on the loose, and people are frightened. But they'll come around. Sooner or later they'll realize that you're innocent."

Talia jumped up from the couch. Her blond hair gleamed in the soft light. "Sooner or later?" She laughed harshly. "How long will that be? A month? A year? Ten years? How long will I have to wait?"

"I don't know," Seth replied honestly. "Only time will tell."

"Well, I can't take it anymore," Talia said fiercely.

Seth sat up on the couch, suddenly on the alert. Something in her tone startled him. She wasn't like herself.

"What do you mean?" he asked.

Talia didn't reply. She laughed softly, then strode across the room. She knelt down in front of a cabinet that stood against the far wall.

She pulled open the bottom doors, reached inside, and took out two mysterious objects. They were round. About the size of coconuts.

What is she doing? Seth wondered.

Talia placed the two objects on a bookshelf and turned to Seth.

"Well?" she asked proudly. "How do you like them? These are my trophies."

Seth stared harder.

It couldn't be.

A strange, hoarse giggle escaped his throat. He jumped to his feet and took a step toward the bookshelf.

Then he froze.

Two human heads stared at him.

The skin was green and shriveled. Patches of hair had fallen off. But Seth recognized them at once.

Shandel and Rudy.

Seth turned to Talia, his mouth open in an *O* of horror.

"I saved them," Talia explained casually. "My trophies."

A long silver object glinted in her hand.

A hacksaw!

Where did she get that?

Seth raised both hands to protect himself.

Talia moved forward with surprising speed, slashing the air with the blade of her hacksaw.

"I need another trophy," she told him.

chapter 23

"No way," Talia declared. Her voice was firm and steady. "I'm not doing it, Seth. There's no way I'm reading that story at tonight's meeting."

"But, Talia—" Seth pleaded.

"Forget it," she snapped. Tears welled up in her eyes. "I can't, Seth. Not after everything that's happened. I can't believe you called a Thrill Club meeting for tonight without discussing it with me. You didn't even tell me why I was coming to your house. And now Maura and Nessa are going to be here any minute. How can you ask me to read them such a horrible story?"

Seth didn't argue. He set the story down on his father's desk. "No problem," he murmured softly. "If you don't want to do it, you don't have to do it. I just thought you might want to read something tonight. For old time's sake. So everyone would know you were okay."

How could he think that? Talia wondered. How could he even *dream* that I might read a story about saving Shandel's and Rudy's heads as trophies? A story in which I admit that I'm an insane murderer?

Sometimes Seth was so insensitive, it was beyond belief!

And what if the police got hold of this story? What if they used it against her in court?

Her hearing was only two weeks away. It would just confirm everything that people thought about her. That she was some kind of heartless, unfeeling monster. A person who killed her friends without the slightest trace of remorse.

Talia slumped on the couch, suddenly exhausted.

The doorbell rang, and Seth rushed out of the room to answer it.

Talia didn't like being alone in Seth's father's study. She glanced around uncomfortably. The walls were cluttered with exotic artifacts from New Guinea—shields, primitive swords and spears, and lots of grotesque masks like the one Seth had worn to her house that night.

This was the room where Dr. Varner had died, Talia remembered with a shudder. Died at his desk of mysterious causes.

Seth returned a moment later with Maura and Nessa in tow. Except for her brief glimpse of Maura from the hospital window, Talia hadn't seen either one of them since she had been taken to St. Elizabeth's.

She couldn't blame them for staring, for trying to figure out if she was the same old Talia, or a new person entirely, a dangerous, psychotic killer.

It's me, she pleaded silently. Talia. Your friend. Please don't hate me.

"Hi," Nessa said warmly. "It's so good to see you, Talia."

"Same here." Talia smiled. She wanted to hug Nessa, but she didn't know if it would make Nessa nervous. She remained seated on the couch. "It's really great to be back."

Maura hung back, hiding partway behind Nessa, tugging nervously at her shirt cuffs.

She's hiding, Talia thought. She's embarrassed to see me. Especially since she's been spending time with Seth behind my back.

"How was the hospital?" Maura asked. "Did they treat you okay?"

"It was fine," Talia replied. "They gave me shock treatments only when I wouldn't eat the food."

She thought it was a pretty good joke—but no one laughed.

It's so tense in here, Talia realized. It's like we're strangers.

"Hey, lighten up, guys!" Seth exclaimed. "This isn't a funeral."

"We've been to too many funerals lately," Maura reminded him, staring at the floor. "I've been to enough funerals in the past month to last forever."

Nessa tucked a strand of brown hair behind her

ear. "I don't know," she said gloomily. "I'm not sure we should have this meeting. After everything that's happened, maybe we should just disband the Thrill Club."

Maura disagreed. "We enjoyed it before. We have to try to enjoy our lives, don't we?"

Talia didn't say anything. She still hadn't gotten over the fact that there were only four of them present. She kept glancing at the doorway, waiting for Shandel and Rudy to arrive.

A Thrill Club reunion.

Seth slid closer to her on the couch. He placed his hand softly on her shoulder. "Talia," he said, loud enough for everyone to hear, "why don't you read your story?"

Talia glanced up in surprise. For a moment she didn't understand what he was talking about. "What story?" she asked.

Seth held a sheaf of papers in his hand. He must have grabbed them from his father's desk on his way back into the room. "This one," he said. "The one you read to me before Nessa and Maura got here."

Talia felt trapped. How could she deny writing the story, when Seth held it in his hand? And how could she refuse to read it?

Why is Seth doing this to me? she wondered.

"I don't feel like it," she said truthfully, hoping that would get her off the hook.

"Go ahead," Nessa said encouragingly. "I've really missed your stories. You're such a great writer."

Talia wished she could tell them the truth. *I didn't write this story, or the last one, or the one before that. Seth did. He's the great writer, not me.*

But if she admitted all that, it would make her seem like a liar—and she needed her friends to believe her right now.

"If you don't feel like reading it," Seth told her, "I'll be happy to read it for you." He tapped the rolled-up story impatiently against his knee. "I think it's really great," he told Maura and Nessa. "One of Talia's best."

Seth, please, Talia thought. Why are you doing this? Why are you being so heartless?

"I was hoping you'd read us a story," Maura added in a surprisingly kind voice.

What can I do? Talia wondered.

Think, she told herself. There has to be a solution.

And suddenly, one came to her. The perfect solution. She would begin the story as Seth had written it, but then change it at the end.

Instead of taking Shandel's and Rudy's heads from the cabinet, I'll just have them be shrunken heads from New Guinea. That will be creepy enough, without hurting anyone's feelings. Seth won't dare complain.

Okay, she thought. Here goes.

Talia took the papers from Seth's hand, cleared her throat, and began to read in a soft, shaky voice: *"Seth chewed his pencil and studied the math problem."*

Once she started, her nervousness disappeared.

The sound of the words soothed her. The power of the sentences.

She saw the scene unfolding in her head. Seth driving over to her house. Sitting down next to her on the couch. Watching as she bent down and opened the cabinet.

"She pulled open the bottom doors, reached inside, and took out two mysterious objects. They were round. About the size of coconuts."

Talia paused to collect her thoughts. Now I have to begin improvising, she told herself. Forget the words on the page.

She glanced up at her audience. Maura and Nessa watched her closely, nervously waiting for the next sentence.

Then she turned her eyes to Seth and noticed something strange. He wasn't even paying attention! He was listening to his Walkman. Moving his lips to some private music. He wasn't listening to a word she said.

I can change anything I want to, she realized. He'll never even know.

Then she blanked out for a second. A sharp buzzing noise erupted inside her head.

"Ow!" she cried.

"What's the matter?" asked Maura.

"Nothing," Talia replied uncertainly.

What's going on here? she wondered. What's this buzzing in my head?

"Keep reading," pleaded Nessa. "I'm dying to know what happens next."

Despite her plans to make up a new ending, Talia began to read the story Seth had written for her.

What's wrong with me? she wondered. Why can't I stop myself?

As she read the frightening scene, she glanced up at Seth. He was watching her now, smiling.

Before she knew it, she had reached the chilling end of the story. *"She moved forward with surprising speed, slashing the air with the blade of her hacksaw. 'I need another trophy.'"*

Feeling shaky, Talia lowered the pages of the story and glanced at her audience.

Maura and Nessa stared back at Talia with wide eyes, their expressions troubled.

"It's a creepy story, Talia," Nessa declared. "But how could you even think of reading it to us? I mean, two of us have died and—"

The buzzing in Talia's head drowned out Nessa's voice.

All at once the buzzing faded—and a voice started speaking in her head.

A new voice. A soft, commanding voice.

The hacksaw, it said. *Go pick up the hacksaw. It's on top of the desk.*

Talia felt herself moving awkwardly across the room. She stopped at the desk.

She reached inside a plain brown shopping bag.

She pulled out a hacksaw.

She ran her fingertips softly over the jagged teeth of the blade.

Good, said the soft voice in her head.

Now go get another trophy.

chapter 24

Her head buzzing, Talia moved stiffly across the room, waving the hacksaw in front of her.

Maura, commanded the voice. *Go to Maura.*

Helplessly, Talia followed the command.

She advanced across the room and stopped in front of Maura, who stared up at her with terrified green eyes.

Talia lowered the hacksaw blade to Maura's neck.

"Stop it, Talia," Maura cried. "This isn't funny."

From the corner of her eye, Talia saw Nessa rise from her seat.

Watch out for Nessa, urged the voice. *Don't let her sneak up on you.*

Moving to obey, Talia turned to threaten Nessa with the hacksaw.

"Sit down, Nessa," Talia heard herself say in a thick, distorted voice. "Unless you want to be next."

Reluctantly, Nessa sat back down. She turned frantically to Seth. "Do something!" Nessa shouted. "There's something wrong with Talia!"

Go get your trophy, ordered the voice in Talia's head.

Talia turned back to Maura, who was cowering in her chair, trying to protect her face and neck from the hacksaw.

Get your trophy—now! the voice commanded.

Talia raised the hacksaw high above her head.

Maura screamed and tried to squirm away.

Talia furiously grabbed a handful of Maura's short red hair. She slashed the blade toward Maura's throat.

But a hand pulled her arm.

Nessa!

"Are you crazy?" Nessa shrieked. "Are you *crazy?*"

Free yourself, said the voice. *Don't let Nessa stop you.*

With a powerful tug, Talia tore herself from Nessa's grasp. She stumbled backward toward Dr. Varner's desk.

"Talia—it really was you!" she heard Nessa scream. Nessa moved to shield Maura with her body. "You really *did* kill Shandel and Rudy!"

Get rid of Nessa, said the voice. *She knows too much.*

Talia obediently charged across the room, grabbed Nessa by the shirt collar, and prepared to take her trophy.

chapter

25

Without hesitating, Talia pressed the sharp teeth of the hacksaw blade against the soft flesh of Nessa's throat.

Now! commanded the voice. *Now!*

Nessa shrieked as Talia slid the blade across her neck.

Talia cried out as Maura slammed into her hard, tackling Talia around the waist.

Talia crashed to the floor with a loud groan.

The hacksaw flew out of her hand. She saw it slide across the floor.

It's under the desk, said the voice in Talia's head. *Tear yourself loose and get it.*

The room whirled crazily as Talia wrestled with Maura on the floor. She wrapped her hands around Maura's throat.

Maura squirmed out of her grasp and fought back ferociously.

Glancing up as she struggled, Talia saw that Seth hadn't moved from his chair. His head was lowered. The headphones were still covering his ears.

The voice spoke inside of Talia's head again. *Come on,* it urged. *You can do better than that.*

Maura gained control, straddling Talia's chest with her knees, pressing down on Talia's arms. Talia gasped for breath. She lay flat on her back, glaring up at Maura from under strands of her loose blond hair.

"Had enough?" Maura, red-faced, panting, demanded.

Play dead, said the voice.

Talia did as she was told. Sensing Talia's surrender, Maura relaxed her grip.

Now! shouted the voice.

With surprising quickness, Talia freed one of her arms and reached up to grab a handful of Maura's red hair. Maura cried out in pain, but she didn't give in. She dug her knees harder into Talia's shoulders until Talia's fingers loosened, releasing Maura's hair.

"Had enough?" Maura asked again.

NOW! the voice commanded. DO IT!

Obediently, Talia arched her back, lifting Maura's knees into the air. With an animal grunt, Talia twisted her body hard.

Maura cried out as she lost her balance and toppled onto the floor.

The desk, said the voice. *The hacksaw is under the desk.*

Talia squirmed free and crawled across the floor toward the desk. Her fingers were within inches of the hacksaw when Nessa came flying across the room, flinging her body on top of Talia's.

Maura scrambled to Nessa's aid. Together, the two girls pinned Talia to the floor.

FIGHT! screamed the voice. YOU CAN DO IT!

Once again Talia struggled violently to free herself, thrashing like a wild animal caught in a trap.

But Maura and Nessa held on.

Talia's body went limp.

This is bad, said the voice. *I'm going to have to handle this myself.*

chapter 26

Talia blinked her eyes and gazed around in confusion.

Where am I? she wondered. What is happening?

"Maura? Nessa? What are you doing?" she asked in a halting voice. "You—you're hurting me. Let me up."

"You're not fooling us," Maura cried breathlessly. "Don't pretend, Talia."

"Ow! Let me up!" Talia protested. "You're hurting my arms!"

The two girls kept her pinned to the floor.

Talia realized she hadn't the strength to fight them. She felt exhausted, completely drained.

"Where's the hacksaw?" Nessa asked.

"Under the desk. She can't reach it," Maura replied.

"Hacksaw?" Talia cried. "What hacksaw? What's happened? Please—let me up!"

"We can't let you up—till the police come," Maura told her. She turned to Nessa. "I can hold her. Hurry—call the police."

Talia lay helpless on the floor as Nessa climbed to her feet and hurried to the phone on the desk.

As she reached for the phone, Seth suddenly came to life. He pulled off his headphones and leapt to his feet.

As he grabbed the receiver from Nessa's hand, his mouth curled into a cruel smile.

"No one escapes tonight," he told them calmly, coldly. "No one escapes."

chapter 27

"No one escapes," Seth repeated, glaring at them.

Talia felt Maura let go of her arm. She sat up, her head spinning.

"Seth?" Talia cried shrilly. "What are you *saying?*"

Seth uttered a harsh laugh. His eyes gleamed excitedly. "Talia—haven't you guessed? Haven't you guessed? My father didn't die. He escaped!"

Talia felt a wave of fear sweep over her.

What is happening? First I wake up on the floor, my entire body aching. And now Seth seems to have totally *snapped!*

"Seth, you're talking crazy," she told him. "Please—calm down. Try to calm down."

Seth wasn't listening. "No one escapes," he muttered again. "No one!"

"Seth, please," Talia begged. "You're not making any sense." Talia watched Maura and Nessa gaping at Seth in open-mouthed confusion.

"My father escaped," Seth repeated, ignoring Talia's pleas. "But no one else."

"Your father *what?"* she asked.

"Escaped," Seth repeated impatiently. "He didn't die. He left us. He *escaped* from us."

"But, Seth," Maura cried in confusion. "You know your father is dead. We were with you at the funeral. He—he's buried in the new cemetery on Old Mill Road."

Talia climbed unsteadily to her feet, her eyes on Seth.

Poor Seth, she thought. He's been so stressed out about his father's death. And now—he's totally lost it.

"Don't move," he told them. He stepped over to the couch and pulled the cassette from his Walkman. Then he crossed the room and shoved the cassette into a tape deck on a shelf above his father's desk.

A few seconds later strange chanting filled the room.

Talia's entire body convulsed in a cold shudder.

She remembered the tape. It was the chanting tape Seth had played for her that night in his room.

Yes. She remembered how the chanting had stuck in her mind, how it had made her feel so strange, so dizzy and weak.

Seth lowered the volume on the tape deck. "My father *did* escape! This is no ordinary tape," he explained. "Don't you remember what it said on the case, Talia? Remember the label on the case?"

"Yes," Talia replied. "It said 'transfer tape.' "

"That's right. It's a transfer tape," Seth replied, staring at her. The emptiness in his eyes gave her a chill.

"It's a *mind* transfer tape, Talia. My father brought it home from the New Guinea tribe he studied. If you join in, if you chant along with the voices, your mind floats free of your body."

Seth let out a bitter sob. "My father played it and escaped to someone else's body—and he never came back."

Seth's eyes got wilder as he continued. "One night I played the tape. I chanted. I found out what the tape can do."

His eyes narrowed. His face contorted in a bitter sneer. "Do you know how much it hurt me when I figured it out, Talia? Do you know how much he hurt me?"

Talia didn't know what to say. She could hear the pain in Seth's voice. But how could she help him? It was all too confusing, too weird.

"Seth," she pleaded. "Sit down. Let's talk about this."

"NO!" Seth shrieked, slamming his fist down on top of his father's desk.

Nessa and Maura cried out in alarm.

He's totally out of control, Talia realized. He could do anything. He could kill us all.

What are we going to do? What?

"So, welcome to the final Thrill Club meeting," Seth said bitterly.

The three girls huddled together as Seth snatched a long New Guinean knife off the wall above the couch and began advancing toward them.

It's me he wants, Talia realized.

Seth raised the blade. "You didn't care about me," he told Talia. "You used me, that's all. Your math homework. Your horror stories. I would have done anything for you. Anything. But you didn't care about me. Only what I could do for you. I knew you were planning to leave me. To leave me, just as my father did!"

Talia stared hard at Seth as he approached. Please, Seth, she pleaded silently. Please don't hurt me.

"Seth, it's just not true," she told him in a trembling voice.

Seth shook his head impatiently. "I know you were ready to dump me for Rudy, Talia. But I couldn't let you do that. I wanted you to need me the way I needed you. I wanted you to depend on me—not just for your stupid math homework."

The ice-cold smile spread across his face. "I had to take drastic measures. So I used the tape. I chanted. I got into your head. I crept into your mind. I made you do all kinds of things!"

Talia's heart pounded in her chest. "What?" she whispered. "What did you make me do?"

"I made you *kill!*" Seth exclaimed excitedly. "Shandel's death gave me the idea. That one was just an accident. I got into your head planning to scare her. But we grabbed the wrong knife. Poor Shandel. I thought we had the joke knife. What a surprise!" Seth laughed wildly.

"But Rudy—he had it coming," he continued, brandishing the long knife. "Rudy wanted to steal you away from me, Talia. When I saw you kissing him that day in the gym, I knew Rudy had to go. I explained it all to Rudy while he choked and thrashed, and his eyes pleaded for mercy!"

Talia went cold all over. So *that's* what happened. That's why I couldn't remember.

She gaped at Seth in horror and disbelief. "You used me to kill my friends?"

Seth nodded, his eyes completely dead. "That's right, Talia. I used *you.* Just the way you used *me!* I floated inside your mind. I was in control—and you didn't even know it!"

Talia couldn't speak. She just stared down at her hands, the hands that had killed Shandel and Rudy.

But *I* didn't do it, she reminded herself. My *hands* did, but *I* didn't.

Seth did it.

Nessa broke the silence. "Seth," she said softly, "please put down the knife. Don't hurt anyone else. We're your friends."

"You need help," Maura added, her voice just above a whisper. "If you put down the knife, we'll see that you get help. Really."

Seth ignored their pleas. He reached for the stereo and turned up the volume. The rhythmic chanting filled the room.

Seth began chanting along in a soft, droning voice.

Cringing, terrified, Talia pressed her fingers to her ears to drown out the frightening sound. "Stop it!" she begged. "Please! What are you doing?"

"The chanting—it's going to kill us all!" Maura screamed.

Nessa covered her ears and shut her eyes. "Stop it! Stop it! Before our minds all float away!"

"Too late—" Seth murmured.

chapter 28

Seth began chanting at the top of his lungs.

"Grab him!" Talia cried. "Stop him!"

Maura leaped forward and grabbed Seth's arm.

The long-bladed knife slid from Seth's hand and bounced harmlessly onto the carpet.

Seth chanted loudly. Then suddenly he stopped.

He gazed wide-eyed at Talia. "Too late," he repeated. "Too late."

She saw his knees buckle. She ran to him.

She and Maura lowered him softly to the carpet. Talia brought her face close to his lips. He wasn't breathing.

His eyes stared up at her. Blank. Lifeless.

His body felt so warm, but she knew he was no longer in there.

"Seth escaped too," Talia murmured. "He isn't coming back. He's dead."

Talia arranged the flowers in a vase and set them in the center of the kitchen table. She paused for a moment to admire the bouquet.

"Thank you," she said. "They're really beautiful. But I told you, it's not my birthday."

Maura grinned. "Well, what else can we celebrate?"

"How about all the charges against me being dropped?" Talia suggested. "I don't think the court believed the truth. But they couldn't prove I killed anyone."

Maura shook her head. "You didn't kill anyone. Seth did. But let's just celebrate the fact that it's Saturday," she said dryly.

"Okay," Talia agreed. "Yaaaay, Saturday!" Her smile faded. "It's hard to forget about all that happened, hard to shut it away."

Maura nodded, agreeing.

"Poor Seth," Talia said. "I miss him. I really do. I know it's strange, Maura, but I think about him the way he was before his father died. Before he changed. He was so smart and caring. That's the Seth I miss."

Maura nodded. "I miss him too, Talia. We used to talk to each other all night. Through our bedroom windows. He could be so funny sometimes."

The room grew silent, each girl deep in her own thoughts.

Maura glanced at her wristwatch. "Uh-oh. I've got to run. Give me a call tonight. Maybe Nessa can join us and we can all go to the movies or something."

"Sounds good," said Talia. She walked her friend to the front door.

"Happy unbirthday," Maura said, stopping on the front stoop.

"Happy Saturday," Talia replied. "Thanks for the flowers. Know what I'm going to do now?"

"What?"

Talia smiled. "I'm going to write another horror story."

Maura's face went pale. "Talia," she said, "are you sure it's a good idea?"

"Don't worry," Talia told her. "I'll make sure this one has a happy ending!"

About the Author

"Where do you get your ideas?"

That's the question that R. L. Stine is asked most often. "I don't know where my ideas come from," he says. "But I do know that I have a lot more scary stories in my mind that I can't wait to write."

So far, he has written nearly three dozen mysteries and thrillers for young people, all of them bestsellers.

Bob grew up in Columbus, Ohio. Today he lives in an apartment near Central Park in New York City with his wife, Jane, and fourteen-year-old son, Matt.

THE NIGHTMARES
NEVER END . . .
WHEN YOU VISIT

Next: ***THE DEAD LIFEGUARD***

Lindsay Beck can't wait to return to North Beach Country Club for her second summer as a lifeguard—a summer of swimming, sunning, and partying in the dorm. But suddenly, being a lifeguard is no longer fun—it's terrifying!

One by one, the lifeguards start dying gruesome deaths. Someone—or something—is out to kill *all* the lifeguards. Can Lindsay figure out the secret behind the evil at the swim club before she becomes the next victim?